DEAL
with IT

Che
to re
ww
ww

DEAL *with* it

ESSENCE BESTSELLING AUTHOR
Monica McKayhan

KIMANI
tru

Recycling programs
for this product may
not exist in your area.

DEAL WITH IT

ISBN-13: 978-0-373-83141-8

© 2009 by Monica McKayhan

www.KimaniTRU.com

Printed in U.S.A.

For my Granny, Rosa A. Heggie
(November 1927–July 2008).

She was special in so many ways, and the strongest woman
I knew. My life is rich because of her.

For all the young men and women who told me that *Indigo Summer* was the first book they read from cover to cover, I think you're awesome! To my sons, nieces, nephews and cousins, who took me back to being a teenager for the sake of the Indigo Summer series. And my family and close friends, who keep me grounded.

one

Indigo

Marcus Carter: handsome, smart, sweet. He'd help you get a better grade in math or give you his jacket in the rain. He'd even buy you a meal if you were hungry. He was close to being perfect, not to mention he was fine. What more could a girl ask for in a boyfriend? At the moment, however, it was hard to see those traits in him because all I wanted to do was wrap my skinny fingers around his neck and choke him.

He stood leaning against the wall, holding on to a foam cup—Terrence Hill standing next to him, with that goofy grin on his face. Terrence was holding a foam cup, too, and they laughed about something funny and talked about everybody who walked past. He and Terrence had become pretty close friends, hanging out just about every day together. They played ball *together,* hung out *together* at the mall on the weekends, went to the skating rink *together.* If I didn't know any better, I would've thought they were going out *together.* I was beginning to wonder if Marcus was my boyfriend or if he was Terrence's.

"Are we riding to the party together or what?" I had asked Marcus just two hours before the party.

He'd hesitated, flashed that beautiful smile. "It would be cool if you could ride with your girls, you know, Jade and them," he'd said, as if I didn't know who my girls were. "Me and Terrence are probably gonna ride together."

Me and Terrence. Me and Terrence. Me and Terrence. I was sick of this me-and-Terrence thing, and I was determined to do something about it one way or another. It was cool for Marcus to have a new friend. After all, he didn't have many friends—he was pretty much a loner. But *hello,* what about his girlfriend who was being kicked to the curb every chance he got?

One time it was for a game of *NBA Live,* no less. Marcus and I were supposed to be studying together, but when I'd showed up at his door, he'd answered wearing a pair of gray sweatpants, a white tank top and a red ski cap on his head. He'd had this stupid grin on his face and a PlayStation controller in his hand. He'd swung the door open and looked at me as if I was the one who was crazy.

"What's up, Indi?" he'd asked.

"Um, we're supposed to be studying," I'd said.

"Oh, yeah," he'd said and smiled. "I almost forgot."

"Almost?" I'd steadied my backpack across my shoulder, stood there for a moment.

"Come on inside." Marcus had swung the door open wider, "I just need a few minutes."

"Hey, man, I need a refill on the soda." Terrence had rushed down the stairs, wearing black sweatpants, a similar tank top and a black ski cap on his head. "Hey, what's up, Indi?"

"Hey, Terrence." I'd glanced at Marcus.

"I just need a minute to finish whipping Hill right quick," Marcus had said.

"In your dreams, Carter," Terrence had said as he swung

Marcus's refrigerator door open like he was at home and refilled his glass with soda.

The two of them had rushed back upstairs like two little kids, and I'd followed close behind. They both sat on the edge of Marcus's bed, leaned forward in front of his television, controllers in their hands. They continued playing *NBA Live,* completely forgetting that I was in the room. I'd sat quietly in a chair in the corner of the room, pulled my math book out and my worksheet and begun to look it over. They'd yelled every time either one of them made a basket. Occasionally, one of them would do a little dance around the room. Before long, a few minutes had turned into an hour, and I was tired of waiting. I'd simply gathered my things, stuffed them into my backpack and slipped out of the room. I'd crept down the stairs and out the front door. Marcus didn't even know I was gone. That was when I knew that I was slowly being replaced by Terrence Hill, and I wasn't at all happy about it.

As I watched Terrence standing next to Marcus like a wallflower at the party, with that smug look on his face, I wondered what Jade had ever seen in him. Chocolate Boy, as she called him, had been her boyfriend for a while. But he'd dumped her for a girl who was much older and in college. She must've been, like, a junior at Spelman by now. When Miss Spelman decided to dump Terrence for someone else, it was then that he discovered that he wanted Jade back.

"Please tell me you're not messing with him again," I said, shivering from the cold as we stepped inside the doors of the community center where the party was being held.

Streamers and balloons hung from the ceiling, along with a banner that read Happy Birthday, Kevin. A long table against the wall held cups filled with fruit punch and a huge birthday cake. The lights were dimmed, and a disco ball hung from the ceiling.

The DJ in the corner of the room encouraged people to dance as he played hip-hop music. Everyone stood against the wall, just looking around at each other, not wanting to be the first to dance. Jade and I had caught a ride with Tameka, who was the only one in our clique with a driver's license. Occasionally, her parents let her get the wheels, and this was one of those times. The three of us made a beeline for the punch table.

"What's wrong with her talking to him again?" Tameka asked. "I think Terrence is a nice guy."

Tameka was probably the worst judge of guys, having gone through at least four boyfriends since the beginning of our freshman year. Her newest boyfriend, Vance Armstrong, was in love with himself and basketball, of course. Girls were constantly in his face, and he loved the attention. It was just a matter of time before he moved on to a new cheerleader or dance-team girl. For some reason, Tameka always thought that each guy she dated would be her knight in shining armor, and they would live happily ever after and drive off into the sunset. Each relationship always ended in disaster, and she'd move on to the next guy, hoping he'd rescue her from…herself, I guess.

As confident as Tameka seemed to be, there was definitely something missing from her life—a void that she tried filling with boys. What was worse was that she usually ended up with shallow guys who cared only about themselves, and she was the one who ended up hurt. And now here she was, giving Jade her two cents about Terrence.

"We're just friends," Jade said. "I don't know why y'all are making a big deal out of it, anyway."

I looked at Jade, her nose red from the cold. She was trying something new with her hair. She had it in microbraids and had pulled it up on top of her head in a sort of ponytail thing. She was wearing makeup, and not just eyeliner and lip gloss, but the real stuff—foundation, mascara and eye shadow. Whenever we visited the mall, she insisted on spending half the day at the MAC counter. Some days she looked twenty-five instead of sixteen. I just wondered if the breakup with Terrence had affected her self-esteem more than she'd let on. Maybe it had her wishing she was older and more mature. Didn't she know that it was okay to just be sixteen? Adulthood was approaching way too fast. Why not just sit back and enjoy the ride? That was what I intended to do.

The music echoed through the community center as boys, with their sagging pants, made hand gestures like rappers and danced around the wall. Everybody wanted to be Lil Wayne. Some even wore the silver grills on their teeth just to imitate his smile. Jade thought that Lil Wayne was the finest boy on the planet next to Usher. I, on the other hand, thought Lil Wayne looked like a cockroach, and I wanted to pull out my can of Raid every time I saw him squirm across the screen in a video.

"It's about time y'all got here," Tymia said, appearing out of nowhere. "This party is whack. Nobody's even dancing."

Tymia, who wore gold lip gloss on her lips and skinny jeans that hugged her hips, was not afraid of anything. She freely spoke her mind, which was why I had instantly liked her. We normally didn't hang out with ninth graders. That was taboo. But when she joined our dance team, I knew exactly why Miss Martin had picked her. She had rhythm. And even though she was a freshman, she sort of grew on us, so we let her hang out. She was new to Atlanta. Her family had moved from Los Angeles over the summer. She wore pink sunglasses on her face and a funky hairdo; you could tell that she was from somewhere else.

Whenever you saw Tymia, Asia was never far behind. A much taller girl, she looked like a black Barbie doll. With every strand of her hair in place, you could easily mistake it for weave. But it was hers. Her clothes were designer fashion, and we immediately knew that she didn't shop at your regular 5.7.9 or Charlotte Russe stores at the mall. She definitely shopped at expensive boutiques. The moment she'd walked into the gym during dance-team tryouts, Jade and I had giggled at the sight of her.

"I think she's lost," Jade whispered.

"She must be looking for the cheerleading tryouts," I whispered back. "She couldn't be looking for our dance team. Not dressed like that."

"Maybe she thought we were auditioning for *America's Next Top Model*," Jade said and laughed. "Tyra ain't here, boo." She said it loud enough for the girl to hear.

"You are so silly." We both fell out laughing in the bleachers.

As Young Jeezy began to echo through the gym, black Barbie stood there, with her head held low, her legs apart and her hands on her hips. Jade and I looked at each other, wondering what this Tyra Banks look-alike knew about Jeezy, first of all. And second of all, where had she learned how to dance like that? She began moving to the music like she knew what she was doing. Jade and I sat there with our mouths wide open as she put some funk into her routine. We were both in awe of her skills, and from that day forward, she became our friend.

"Let's get this party started right," Asia announced as she marched into the party, wearing one of her designer outfits. "We are not about to stand up against the wall like the rest of these fools in here."

She led the way to the dance floor as Jade, Tameka, Tymia and I followed. Gathered in a circle, we moved our hips to the music. As the sound resonated through the room, I looked around at my girls and realized just how close the five of us had become since the beginning of the year. Our circle on the dance floor was similar to our circle of friendship—harmonious, in step and unbreakable. As we danced together, it wasn't long before others started to crowd the dance floor.

"Can I dance with you?" a deep voice behind me said.

Marcus wrapped his arms around my waist from behind, kissed my neck.

"Why don't you dance with Terrence?" I teased. "Ain't that your new boo?"

"Terrence is not as pretty as you," he said.

As Marcus and I faced each other and began moving to the music, I noticed his hair was shorter.

"New haircut?" I asked, remembering how I used to go to the barbershop with him some afternoons and on Saturday mornings. It was something we did together. Although it wasn't comfortable sitting in a shop filled with men talking about things that only men talked about—football, women and other trash—it was my way of hanging out with Marcus.

"My boy Terrence cut it." He grinned. "I didn't even know he could cut. He did a pretty good job, huh?" He ran his hand across his head.

"It's a'ight," I said, secretly thinking that it looked way better than Marcus's regular haircut.

"Why you be hatin' on my boy like that, Indi?" Marcus asked. "What's up with that?"

"I'm not hatin' on him. I'm just saying."

"He's not gonna take your place or nothing." He laughed. "Don't be jealous."

"I'm not jealous!" I lied.

The truth was, the green-eyed monster had reared its ugly head once again. I *was* jealous. Marcus had always been somewhat of a loner, until I came into his life. I'd filled that empty void, and it felt funny having to share that spot with someone else. It seemed that Marcus was not only spending all of his time with Terrence, but he was also spending all of what should've been my time with Terrence. We barely studied together anymore, barely went to the mall or watched our favorite DVDs over and over anymore. I couldn't remember the last time Marcus took me to a movie or to the Varsity for a burger.

"You have your circle of friends, Indi," he said. "I don't get jealous when you hang out with Danity Kane over there."

"I'm not spending every minute of the day with them," I said.

"I like Terrence. I think he's cool. And he doesn't have many friends. He's had a hard time. You know that, Indi. Having to raise his little brother and sister like that…"

I knew Terrence's story. His mother had been strung out on drugs, and Terrence had been left with the responsibility of taking care of his younger brother and sister. That was, until his mother finally got it together. She went into rehab and turned her life around. I even heard that she had a steady job and was going to church on Sundays. Everybody thought that Terrence was weird, because he was so mysterious, but the truth was, he didn't want everybody in his business. People gave you a hard time when they found out that your mama was a crackhead. The crackhead jokes never ended, so I understood why he kept to himself. But the truth was, Marcus was always befriending weird people. I guess it was because he had a big heart, which was why I loved him in the first place. He never saw things the way the rest of the world did. He always looked at life through a different set of eyes.

I glanced over at Terrence, who was now dancing with Jade. They grinned at each other, and I wondered what they could possibly be talking about that would make them grin like that.

"He better not hurt my friend again," I warned Marcus.

"Indi, I can't control what happens with Jade and Terrence," Marcus said. "Besides, they're just friends, anyway."

"They look like more than just friends to me." I glanced over at Jade and Terrence again as the two of them danced closely, gazing into each other's eyes.

Marcus wrapped his arms around me, pulled me close.

"Indi, you worry about stuff too much."

"I'm worried more about you and me and what's gonna happen when Terrence moves his things into your house."

"You are silly." Marcus smiled, touched the tip of my nose with his fingertip.

When Marcus's lips touched mine, I closed my eyes and savored the moment. I knew that as of late, times like these were few and far between. Who knew when Marcus would have time to hold me like this again?

two

Tameka

with cotton stuffed in between both our sets of toes—one set tangerine with yellow tips and one set lime-green with pink tips—we shared a hot-fudge sundae with whipped cream and a cherry on top. With Tyler Perry's *Why Did I Get Married?* on mute and Alicia Keys playing on the stereo, Mommy flipped through the latest edition of *Essence* magazine while I searched through a copy of *Vibe,* just looking at the pictures.

"I want my hair like this," I told her, pointing to a photo of Mya.

"Last week you wanted it like Rihanna's, and the week before that, you wanted it like Keyshia Cole's hair," she said and laughed. "How do you really want your hair, sweetie?"

"I want it like this," I said, pointing at Mya's photo again.

"I like your hair the way it is, Tameka." Mommy rubbed her hand across my flat-ironed curls. "You just need your ends clipped a little bit. The next time we go see Cynthia, I'll make sure she clips your ends. I made an appointment for Thursday, so you need to come straight home after dance-team practice that day."

"I will, Mommy."

Dance-team practice was the highlight of my life. Being on the dance team was the best thing going. Other girls wanted to be in my shoes, but not every girl was cut out to be on the team. Our dance coach, Miss Martin, had picked only the cream of the crop. She got you as a freshman, and most girls remained on the team throughout their entire high school careers, provided they kept their grades decent and stayed out of trouble. You weren't allowed to get suspended from school under any circumstances. There was also an unspoken rule about managing your weight, so you had to be in shape, too.

"You think I can get a tattoo right here, on my back?" I asked Mommy, pointing to the small of my back, just above my panty line.

"Maybe when you're seventeen."

"Daddy said I could get one when I turned sixteen," I told her.

"I don't think he knew where you were trying to put it," Mommy said.

"It doesn't really matter where I put it," I said.

"I don't know, Tameka. Are you sure you want something permanent like that on your body at all?" she asked.

"Are you serious? You have two tattoos, Mom! You have Daddy's name plastered right across your arm." I touched her arm and pointed it out to her, as if she didn't remember.

"That's exactly why I'm asking if you're sure about it. Tattoos are permanent. And if you're thinking about putting someone's name on your body, then you should think again."

"Mommy, you don't need to worry. I'm not thinking about tattooing Vance's name anywhere on my body," I said. "I'm just talking about a simple little flower or something."

She exhaled. Probably relieved that I wasn't planning on tattooing my boyfriend's name on my back or on my thigh somewhere. Although Vance was the most serious boyfriend that I had ever

had, I knew that relationships were not always permanent—
tattoos *were*. And even though we'd already talked about spending
our lives together and how many kids we were gonna have, I
knew that anything could happen between now and then.

When I was in the ninth grade, I thought that Jeff Donaldson
was the only man on the face of the earth. But that soon changed
when he started going out with someone else. It was Vance who
came along and mended my broken heart. He was sweet and also
smart. In fact, he was the only guy I'd ever dated whose grade-
point average was higher than mine. He took all of the college-
bound courses in school and consistently made the honor roll.
He played basketball and was headed for a full scholarship to
Duke, although Duke wasn't really his college choice. It was his
father's. Dr. Armstrong had received a full ride to Duke when he
was our age, and wanted the same for his son. He pretty much
insisted that Vance attend there simply because it was his alma
mater. Vance wanted to explore other schools, like Georgia State
or Grambling, but his father wasn't hearing any of that. And
besides, scouts from Duke were already watching him. They were
posted up at all the games and had even sent Vance a letter, asking
if he was interested in their school. He wanted to go to college,
but he wished he had the freedom to make his own choices.

At least he had goals.

I had them, too. I planned on attending Spelman, maybe not
on a full scholarship like Vance, but I would at least try and compete
for a few of the smaller ones. I would do my best on the SATs and
see how far that got me, too. Spelman had been my college of
choice since I was in Girl Scouts in the fifth grade. My Girl Scouts'
troop leader had graduated from Spelman, and it was all she talked
about. She'd told us about all the wonderful things that she had
experienced there. She had been one part of my inspiration—that
and the fact that Rudy from *The Cosby Show* had graduated from
there, too. The other part of my inspiration was Mommy.

My mother never had the chance to attend college. In fact, she never finished high school. She was pregnant at sixteen and was married to my dad soon after that. Before she knew it, she had become a young wife and mother all at the same time, and any hopes and dreams that she had were immediately flushed down the toilet. Therefore, going to college was not an option for me; it was something that had to be done—for both Mommy and me.

"Now here's a hairdo that you could really rock, Tameka." Mommy pointed to a photo of Fantasia, with her spiked haircut, and giggled.

"Oh, you got jokes," I said and stuffed a huge spoonful of the sundae into my mouth. "I'm not trying to cut my hair."

"I might cut mine," Mommy announced, her shoulder-length locks bouncing onto her shoulders. She was never afraid to try new things. She would go bald just to see if she liked it, and her hair would grow back, as if nothing had ever changed. "I might get me one of those cute little sassy hairdos for the spring."

"You can't cut your hair! What would Daddy think?" I shrieked.

"He would think that I'm a grown woman who can do whatever she wants to do with her hair." She grabbed the spoon from my hand, dipped it into the sundae and stuffed a huge spoonful of ice cream into her mouth.

My mother was so confident. She didn't care what people said or thought about her. She did what she wanted to do and always spoke her mind. With a body like a twenty-one-year-old, she rocked Apple Bottoms jeans, tight-fitting shirts and wedge-heeled shoes like nobody's business. She knew all the latest dances, had all the latest music and was completely in love with Usher. She kept saying that if he was just a little bit older and she was a little younger, she would holler at him.

Every day, like clockwork, we watched *106 & Park,* and we never missed an episode of *Baldwin Hills.* Sometimes having a conversation with Mommy was like talking to one of my girl-friends at school. She was just that cool. I often wondered what attracted her to my daddy, because he was the complete opposite: he was quiet and never said what was really on his mind, not until it had time to fester. Then it would come out the wrong way. Mommy was always telling him that if he wasn't careful, he was going to wind up with an ulcer. "You have to tell people off right then and there, not wait until you're seeing red," she would say. "By that time, it's too late."

Daddy spent hours working at the studio. Life as a music producer required many hours of work with artists and a strong dedication to the music. Some nights he didn't even come home. But he was strict about my grades and made sure that my clothes were appropriate before I left the house. He didn't like the idea of my dating boys, but he lived with it. It wasn't unusual for him to intercept my calls and give a boy the third degree before handing over the phone. Daddies were like that. They didn't play when it came to their baby girls.

My cell phone, which was on the coffee table, buzzed, and I reached for it.

"Oh, no!" Mommy yelled. "You can't answer that. We're having our girl time, and we said we weren't answering any phones today."

"*You* said we weren't answering any phones today. I never said that," I reminded her. "Besides, it's just a text message, Mommy. It might be from Vance."

She grabbed the phone, and I wrestled her to get it from her, but she was strong. Before long we were on the floor, wrestling over my phone and giggling. When she finally got it away from me, she rushed into the kitchen and I followed. She flipped my cell phone open and began reading my text message, invading my privacy.

I need U. She read aloud. "What does he mean, he needs you?"

"Mom, it's not cool to read other people's text messages."

"No, what's not cool is for a seventeen-year-old boy to be texting my daughter, talking about how he needs her!"

Was she serious?

"Mommy, you can need people in different ways. Maybe he just needs to talk or something," I lied. I knew exactly what Vance needed, because we had just talked about it until two o'clock in the morning. He needed me in an intimate way. "Can I please have my phone?"

He claimed that everybody who was anybody was having sex, and the fact that we weren't having it bothered him. "No pressure," he'd said just before hanging up, "but I really need you, Tameka."

Those were the words that had been stuck in my head until I finally dozed off at four o'clock in the morning. The thought of sex had me shaking in my boots. Not because I was afraid to do it—because I had done it before—but because of the consequences of it. I had done it with Jeff, who had promised that we would be together forever. But the truth was, our forever had ended last semester. My virginity was gone, with nothing left to show for it—no fairy-tale wedding like we'd planned. No big house and three kids after we'd both graduated from college. Nothing. I'd sworn that the next time I gave it up to someone, it would be when I was grown and married. I was afraid to tell Vance that, afraid that the words "until we get married" would scare him away. So instead, I danced around the issue. Hoped that he would forget all about it, and we could just go on with our lives and not have to talk about it.

"You know what we've always talked about, Tameka. You don't let nobody into your pocketbook until you're good and ready...." Mommy finally handed my phone over. She didn't know that someone had already been in my pocketbook and had stolen everything in it.

She had this thing about girls having sex with boys—she thought that teenagers should practice abstinence. Like that would ever happen in the real world. Just because she got pregnant with me when she was sixteen didn't mean that every teenager in the world would wind up pregnant, too.

"There are diseases, or worse, pregnancy. Can you afford to bring a child into this world, Tameka? You're still a child yourself."

I'd heard this speech a million times, and a million times I'd had to convince her that I knew what I was doing. That I wouldn't wind up with HIV/AIDS or some nasty venereal disease. And more than anything, I wouldn't wind up pregnant. The times that Jeff and I did it, we always used protection. So why was she worrying?

"Tameka, I want only what's best for you. I can't live your life for you, but I can teach you what's right. I know my life hasn't been the best example. Hey, I was pregnant at sixteen and then married shortly thereafter. I never finished high school, never got to go to college, missed a lot of parties and fun." She was getting way too serious now. "I don't regret having you, sweetie. I love you to death, and I'm glad you're here. And I don't even regret marrying your father. We have a great life together, and he's a wonderful husband. But I regret not having a say in my life. The choices were already made for me."

I'd lost count of how many times I'd heard this speech. It had been branded into my memory since the age of twelve. I could repeat it verbatim, but she insisted on telling it to me over and over again.

"Okay, so I didn't mean to put a damper on our girls' day, but I had to get that out," she sighed. "You feel me, though?"

"I feel you, and I'm not doing anything stupid."

Instead of replying to Vance's text message, I just shut my phone.

Dressed in matching flannel pajamas from Victoria's Secret, Mommy and I spent the rest of the afternoon slumming—talking about hairstyles and stuffing our faces. I know she didn't mean to put a damper on the day, but the damage was already done.

three

Vance

BASKETBALL practice was different today. As we scrimmaged with the junior varsity team, our nerves were on edge because somebody had said there was a scout in the bleachers, checking out our practice. He was the same dude that I'd spotted at our homecoming game, and then again, at our game against Forest Hill two Fridays before. He wore the Grambling team colors—a gold cap with a black G in the center of it and a black-and-gold polo underneath a blazer.

He sat in the bleachers, his legs propped up, crossed and resting on the bleacher in front of him. Relaxed and leaning back on his elbows, he didn't even flinch when I hit my famous three-pointer. And I tried not to even look his way as I jogged backward down the court to post up for defense. The next time I took the ball down court, I caught the guy pulling a pen and a small notepad out of the pocket of his blazer, writing some notes and then stuffing the pen and pad back into his pocket. I knew then that he was definitely a scout. And pretty soon he quietly eased out of the doors of the gym, like Clark Kent did when he was about to change into Superman. Smooth.

I wasn't sure if he was interested in me, but I was definitely interested in a free ride at Grambling State University. It wasn't my father's school choice for me, but it was definitely mine. He wanted me to be a Duke man like him. I wanted to explore my options, check out some of the historically black colleges, like FAMU, Howard University or Grambling State. Some of dad's old college buddies were now professors at Duke. And his ex-roommate was one of the head basketball coaches. He'd been watching my game since I was in middle school, and had already promised me a free ride, with all the perks. But attending a school where all of Daddy's buddies were my professors and basketball coaches meant twenty-four-hour surveillance, and I wasn't having that. But I wasn't sure how I was going to break the news to Dad that I had my eye on Grambling.

When I mentioned it before, he'd said, "Now why in the world would you even consider that little country school in Louisiana? You gotta think bigger than that, son! Grambling's too small for you."

"I haven't settled on Duke yet, Dad," I'd said to him at the beginning of basketball season. "I'm exploring my options."

He hadn't been happy with that comment. He'd frowned, raised the *Atlanta Journal-Constitution* up to his nose and begun reading. He was done talking to me, and I felt dismissed. I never brought the conversation up again. Instead, I continued to give my game the best I could, and hoped for other offers.

I tried to keep my focus on school and on my game, but it was hard to focus when girls were constantly jocking you. They showed up at practice, they lingered after the games, they called your house at ungodly hours of the night and they stalked you at school. There was nowhere to turn, even when you told them that you had a girlfriend. That only made them want you more, which made my current girlfriend, Tameka, want to fight the entire female population.

Tameka had been my girl since the beginning of basketball season. We had chorus together during the first semester, and since she was on the dance team, we would see each other after school a lot. I never really paid much attention to her until she asked me for a piece of gum one day.

"You got some gum?" she'd asked, a pair of leotards hugging her hips as we both sat in the bleachers.

"I got Trident." I smiled.

"Trident?" She frowned. "You ain't got no Bubblicious or Bubble Yum?"

"No. I chew Trident. It's sugar free. Better for your teeth," I told her as I pulled the package out of my pocket. "You want one or not?"

"Yeah, I'll take one. It's better than nothing." She pulled a piece of Trident out of the package and popped it into her mouth. "Thanks."

"You're a pretty good dancer. I saw you out there practicing earlier," I told her. "You been dancing long?"

"Forever," she said. "What about you? Can you dance?"

"I can get down a little bit." I'd smiled. She had my attention immediately, and I wasn't sure why. I guessed it was her straightforward attitude, or maybe it was the way she wore those leotards. "Why do you ask?"

"There's a party on Saturday night at this teen club on Jonesboro Road. You going?"

I hadn't been to a party in a long time. After all, I was a busy man—basketball, school and working part-time in my father's dental practice left me little time for extracurricular activities.

"I hadn't really thought about it, but if you're going…yeah, I'll probably go." I blushed as she pulled a piece of lint from my eyebrow and brushed her fingertips across my face. She was so natural with me. I felt comfortable with this girl.

I wanted to ask her what the name and complete address of the club were, and what time the party would start. I wanted to ask what I should wear, but I decided that questions like that would make me seem silly—like I was uncool or didn't know my way around a high school party.

"Cool." She smiled. "Maybe I'll see you there." She threw her gym bag across her shoulder, left the bleachers and headed for the door. I knew then that she would be my girl.

That was four months ago, and we'd been like Elmer's glue and construction paper ever since. Stuck. That is, until the new girl at school, Darla Union, walked into my American history class. I couldn't take my eyes off her. She had cute little dimples and a set of crystal-white teeth, which my father would appreciate, and she wore her hair in long curls and reminded me of Alicia Keys. She wore jeans that were glued to her hips and a top that clung to her vanilla skin. She even looked like she worked out at the gym, because her arms were a little muscular, like Angela Bassett's were in Tyler Perry's movie *Meet the Browns*.

She stared as she took a seat at the desk next to mine. I stared, too, because I was mesmerized by her beauty.

"You got an extra pencil?" she whispered, opening her American history book to the page that Mr. Harris was teaching from.

"Yeah." I handed her the worn-down, chewed-up number-two pencil that I'd picked up at my father's dental office.

She looked at the pencil as if it had cooties, twirled it around and read the black letters on it: Armstrong Dental—Smile Brighter! "Thanks." She smiled when she caught me watching.

"What's your name?" I asked.

"Darla. What's yours?" She smiled that smile again.

"Vance." I stuck my chest out. "Vance Armstrong." I was sure that she'd heard my name before. After all, everybody in our student body knew me. I was a superstar—the LeBron James of Carver High School. Surely she'd heard all the hype.

"Nice to meet you, Vance Armstrong."

That was it.

At that point she took a nosedive into her American history book and never returned. She was one of the few people who actually took notes during Mr. Harris's lecture. Maybe it was because she was brand-new, but she listened intently to his monotone voice, which normally put everyone else to sleep. Darla seemed carefree and so sure of herself. She was nothing like the other girls I knew; they were all so needy and shallow. Not Darla. She didn't even care that I was sitting there, staring at her, as she ferociously recorded every syllable that Mr. Harris spoke.

There was no doubt in my mind—I wanted to know her better. But having a girlfriend definitely made that tricky. The problem was, I happened to actually like my girlfriend, unlike some of my friends on the team, who dated girls for one reason and one reason only. Tameka was smart, funny and had a nice body, too. I enjoyed talking to her on the phone until the wee hours of the morning—even on school nights. And she definitely knew her way around a dance floor and could skate her behind off—backward, too. Not to mention her pops was a music producer. I was just waiting for my opportunity to free-style for him since the first time Tameka told me what he did for a living. She'd promised to tell him about my lyrics. And I knew that once he heard me flow, he'd talk to his people, and I'd be on my way to a multimillion-dollar contract. After that, I wouldn't even need a full ride to college. I wouldn't even need to go to college, as a matter of fact. My parents would be disappointed, but they'd get over it after I started throwing cash their way. Mom could get that two-story mini mansion in Buckhead that she'd been eye-balling since they'd posted a For Sale sign in the front yard.

When I was smaller, she would wake up at the crack of dawn

on Saturday mornings. She would scour the garage sales in the areas where rich people lived, like Buckhead. My father was a dentist who made good money. Mom was an attorney who made a nice salary, too, yet she still shopped at garage sales. What was the point in buying other people's junk when you had good junk of your own? I never understood that.

"We're not moving to Buckhead," my dad kept telling her. "We're staying right here in College Park. Keep our money in this community."

That was the end of that. My father had a way of putting his foot down, and nobody asked any questions once he did. He was often unfair with his reasoning and usually responded with, "Because I said so." And because he said so, it was so. It was like that when we discussed my future and college plans. In his mind, I was destined to be a Duke man. He'd graduated from Duke and went on to become a dentist. Therefore, it was in the stars that I graduate from Duke and become a dentist. There weren't any other options, not according to Dad. Most days it depressed me to think about it, so I tried not to.

Marcus Carter threw me a pass, and I headed down court. With the scout from Grambling gone, I could relax a little bit. As I took a shot from the three-point line and the ball hit the backboard and popped off of the rim, I thought, life can be so bittersweet sometimes.

After practice I waited for Tameka to get changed and meet me out front. Most nights I drove her home, and sometimes we stopped at McDonald's and grabbed a burger. Tonight wouldn't be one of those nights, because I was exhausted. I hoped that my mother had prepared something good for dinner, like my favorite, chicken tortilla soup, or my second favorite, spaghetti with meatballs. It was cold enough for a meal like that, and I needed something to stick to my ribs. I zipped my coat up and braced for the cold. Tameka came rushing toward me, her jacket wide open, her gym bag flung across her shoulder, with a sock hanging out of it, and her shoes untied.

"What's up with you?"

"I almost had a fight in the locker room," she said.

"What?" I was shocked.

"This girl Darla was in there talking trash!" she exclaimed. "I don't even know why she was in our locker room. She's not even on the dance team."

The minute she said Darla's name, I didn't hear anything else she said. I immediately visualized those jeans Darla wore in my American history class, and that smile. I couldn't imagine her in a catfight with my girlfriend.

"Let's go before I have to hurt somebody." Tameka pushed the glass doors open, and a cool breeze rushed inside.

She walked briskly toward the parking lot, and once she made it to my car, she stood there, with her arms folded, until I hit the locks. She hopped into the passenger seat, snapped her seat belt on and folded her arms across her chest again. "I can't stand girls like that. They think they're so tough when they're with their girls. But I bet if I had her in a corner by herself, she wouldn't have been talking all that trash."

Tameka ranted the whole way home, and I wondered if Darla was somewhere ranting to her boyfriend, too. Did she even have a boyfriend? And if she did, what would he be like? I wondered if I was her type, or if she even liked athletes. She probably liked nerdy dudes who competed on the debate team or something.

The smell of chicken tortilla soup filled the house as I stepped inside, dropped my backpack on the kitchen floor. I would know that smell anywhere.

"Uh-uh. Take that on upstairs to your room," Mom said, referring to my backpack.

I kissed her cheek as she poured hot water into a mug for tea.

"Hey, Ma," I said.

"How was practice?" she asked.

"Usual," I said, even though it was everything but usual. I changed the subject. "How did it go in court this morning?"

"Pretty good. The guy got off with probation and community service, so that was a victory for me."

My mom was a great attorney. When I was a little boy and she wasn't able to get a babysitter, she'd drag me along to the courthouse, and I'd sit in the back of the room and watch her work her magic. Even back then, I knew she was good, defensive and sharp. Whatever they brought her way, she had a comeback for it. She would wear the prosecution down and end with a victory every time. I was proud of her. Admired her. I had decided long ago that I wanted to be an attorney just like my mother. My father wanted me to be a dentist, but the truth was, I'd already fallen in love with the law. I liked just watching how cool the judge was, sitting up there on the bench with his black robe on and a gavel in his hand. He had the power to change lives, to send people to prison, if that was what he chose to do. And he could determine how long they stayed in prison, too—three years, twenty years, life. Whatever he wanted to do, the power was in his hands. He just looked so cool, in control. I wanted to be an attorney and then eventually become a judge.

Mom would always encourage me. "You can be whatever you want to be, baby," she'd say. "And you don't even have to decide today. You can decide later. Right now, you just keep your grades up and stay focused. Your future is in your hands."

Oh, yeah? Try telling my dad that.

"That's cool. I'm glad you won your case," I said.

"I made your favorite. Chicken tortilla soup." She smiled. "Why don't you go on upstairs and get cleaned up, and I'll fix you something to eat."

"Okay," I said. "A scout from Grambling was at my practice today."

"Really?" She smiled.

"Mom, I really wanna go there. I'm not really interested in Duke."

"I know that, honey." She touched my face. "Things will work out in your favor."

"You think so?" I asked, really wanting an answer. She had always been my biggest cheerleader, my encourager.

"I know so." She smiled. "Now go say hello to your father. He's in his office."

I took the stairs two at a time. Once at the top, I peeked into Dad's office.

"Hey, Dad." I announced my presence.

He was reclined in his chair, his feet on top of the desk, a newspaper in his hand. "Hey, son. Come on in. How was school?"

"It was cool."

"Have a seat."

I took a seat in the chair on the other side of my father's desk, the side where his patients usually sat either before or after he'd pulled their teeth or performed dental procedures that were too painful to think about.

"Check this out. That Elliott Williams kid is something else." He handed me the newspaper to read the article myself.

I looked at the picture of Elliott Williams, Duke's guard from Memphis, going up for a layup. I scanned the article, which talked about Williams's high school years at some school in Tennessee, where he averaged 24.7 points, 7.2 rebounds and 7.1 assists for a 24–3 team; and about how he was voted Tennessee's Mr. Basketball. The article also said that he maintained a 3.7 grade-point average, which was about like mine. Colleges were going crazy trying to recruit him.

"The Blue Devils are lucky to have that boy," Dad said.

"He had other choices, though," I reminded him. "He could've gone to Memphis, Virginia, Clemson. They all wanted him."

"But he chose Duke," Dad said, right before his phone rang. "Now what does that say about the school?"

When Dad answered his phone, I tried to excuse myself from his office, but he motioned for me to stay. I patiently waited as he finished his conversation.

Once he hung up, he said, "Your mom and I are going to Philly this weekend to see your grandmother. We need to make some decisions about her health, review her medicines and make sure she's taking the right things. Besides, she's missing us like crazy."

"Yeah, I miss her, too," I said.

My grandmother was aging quickly. Just last year she'd been traveling to places like Las Vegas and the Caribbean with her friends. Then, after her stroke, she could barely even talk. She didn't seem like the same grandmother who used to take me to the corner deli in Philly for a real Philadelphia cheesesteak when I was a little boy, or to a 76ers game at the Wachovia Center. Nobody was a bigger 76ers fan than her.

"Anyway, we are leaving early Friday morning and will probably be back on Sunday night. That should get you and Lori back in time for school on Monday."

"Do I have to go?" I asked. "I have a game on Friday night, and I really can't miss it."

"Your grandmother is really looking forward to seeing you, son. She hasn't seen you since Thanksgiving."

"I know, Dad. And I really miss her, but this is important to me. If anybody would understand, it would be Grandma. She understands basketball," I pleaded.

"You're right about that," Dad agreed. "I don't see why you have to go. You can stay," he said. "I just need for you to handle yourself in a responsible manner while we're gone. Take care of the house like a man."

Staying home alone was nothing new to me. I'd done it before.

"Is Lori going with you guys?" I asked. My weekend would be destroyed if my little sister was staying home with me.

"Yes, Lori's going," Dad said. "You'll be here by yourself. Are you okay with that?"

"I'm fine with that."

Dad's phone buzzed again.

"I gotta take this," he said, "but we'll talk later."

I excused myself and went down the hall to my bedroom. Excited about the fact that I would have the whole house to myself for an entire weekend, my adrenaline started flowing. What could be better than this? I dropped my backpack in the middle of the floor and fell backward onto the bed. I was tired. Practice was exhausting. Coach had acted like he had an attitude with us or something, and we all felt it. I shut my eyes for a moment. I needed a shower bad just to soothe my aching muscles, but I didn't even feel like turning it on. I couldn't move.

"Mom said come and eat, stupid." Lori popped her head inside my doorway.

I looked up and glared at my sister. Her best friend, Nina, stood next to her.

"Hi, Vance." Nina waved and smiled.

"Hey, Nina." I gave her a nod.

"Ooh, did something die in here? It stinks!" Lori said. "You need to clean up this rat hole."

"Get out!" I yelled. I wasn't in the mood for my sister and her stupidity.

"You'd better get downstairs and eat," Lori said and then disappeared. A few seconds later she appeared in the doorway again. "Right now."

Nina, who stood next to her, giggled and waved again. Twelve-year-old girls were silly.

My body wanted to hop in the shower. My mind told me

to get up. My stomach growled and wanted food. But I couldn't move. I lay there, completely clothed—coat and all—my eyes facing the ceiling. When my cell phone buzzed, I knew it was Tameka calling, but I didn't even have the energy to pull the phone out of my pocket.

Before long I had drifted off to a point of no return.

four

Indigo

There were stop lines, no-passing lines, crosswalk lines, edge lines, lane lines—too many lines to remember which was which—but I did the best that I could. Daddy patiently sat in the waiting area as I took the written exam for my learner's permit. He'd spent lots of time over the past few weeks preparing me for this, going over the driver's manual and quizzing me on the rules and regulations found inside. He'd also allowed me to practice driving a few times in the school's parking lot. And he hadn't fussed very much when I ran over the orange cones while trying to parallel park.

"Driving takes practice, Indi," he'd kept saying.

Driving also took coordination. And coordination I had. After all, I was a member of the hottest dance team in the Atlanta metro area. I knew how to move one part of my body while moving another part at the same time. But for some reason, when it came to moving the front tires of a car in the opposite direction of the steering wheel in order to parallel park, I had absolutely no coordination whatsoever. The good thing was, I knew the driver's manual inside and out: I had studied it every day since the beginning of the school year. And that was all I needed for a learner's permit. By the time I turned seventeen, I would have parallel parking down to a science. I was already enrolled in drivers' ed for the upcoming summer, so there I would learn all the ins and outs of maneuvering a car.

I took a seat next to Daddy in the waiting area and dug deep into my Baby Phat purse in search of a piece of gum. I popped my last piece of Big Red into my mouth and glanced up at the huge clock on the wall. It was ten o'clock on a Saturday morning, and I was just minutes away from being legally able to drive in the state of Georgia—that is, as long as there was an adult in the car. I didn't care that it wasn't a full-blown driver's license. A permit was good enough for now. I could hardly sit still in my chair, thinking about it. All I needed was a fly photo, I thought as I pulled my compact out and took a glance in the mirror. My hair was okay. I dabbed on a bit of lip gloss, smacked my lips together and rubbed a little bit of sleep from the corner of my eye with my fingernail.

I tucked the compact away, sat up straight in my chair and asked Daddy, "So, can I drive us home?"

"Hmm." He thoughtfully placed his finger on his chin. "You think you can handle that, Indi? Home is a long way from here. It's not like driving in the school's parking lot, and it's not our regular practice route."

"Daddy, I have to learn how to drive on regular roads if I'm ever going to get my license," I said. "Of course I can handle it."

"Well, you know there are some tricky twists and turns between here and home."

"Daddy, it's a straight shot."

"But there's that left turn on Jonesboro Road. You know, the one right there at the BP station," he said. "And that's a pretty busy intersection right there by the Rib Shack."

"You worry too much. I can handle it."

"Well, if you think you can handle it—" Daddy smiled nervously "—then I guess you can drive us home."

Yes! I exclaimed silently, where only God and I could hear. I didn't say it out loud, because I didn't want Daddy thinking I was too excited, too eager. I had to appear calm and in control. "That's cool. Don't worry. I'll get you home safe and sound."

I gave the woman behind the counter a subtle smile as she snapped my picture. Didn't want my smile to be too big. I wanted to be laid-back and have a somewhat sexy look on my face. After all, I would be using the permit as ID, too. There was no telling who might be checking out my photo. When she handed me the laminated piece of plastic, I wanted to skip to the car. I couldn't resist showing it off to the nerdy girl with braces who had sat next to me during the exam. Both of us had nervously toiled over the answers to the multiple-choice questions. Now she sat nervously next to her mother in the waiting area.

"Got mine," I told her, with a huge smile on my face. "What about you?"

She dropped her head. "I didn't pass."

"For real?" I felt bad for her. "You know you can always take it again."

"I know. I'll have to come back another day," she said. "But congratulations to you, though."

"Thanks," I said, and then I gave her a smile and followed Daddy to the parking lot.

He tossed me the keys to the truck, and I hopped into the driver's seat. I looked serious as I adjusted my mirrors, strapped on my seat belt and put the truck in Reverse. Daddy was pretending not to be nervous, but I could see in his eyes that he was as he pulled his seat belt across his huge stomach. He was shaking in his boots, probably wishing he had a brake and accelerator on the passenger's side. He adjusted the heat to knock the chill off. The leather seats were cold against my behind as I carefully pulled out into traffic. At the light I hit the brake too hard and sent both of us toward the dashboard.

Daddy glanced over at me. "Remember to hit the brake gently, and start slowing down before you get to the light."

He was so calm. I was so proud of him. He was a much better passenger than Mama was. She was always yelling when I did something wrong, and that only made me more nervous. But Daddy was a trouper. He sat there pretending to be unshaken.

"Sorry, Daddy," I said and made a mental note to work on braking gently.

As I pulled the truck into our driveway, I noticed Marcus standing on his front porch, watching. The hood of his sweat-shirt covered his head, and his hands were stuffed into the pockets. He smiled my way and then walked over to the truck and opened my door.

"Hello, Mr. Summer," he said to Daddy.

"Hey there, Marcus." Daddy smiled and stepped out of the truck on the passenger's side. "She did it," he said with pride. "She got her permit."

"I don't believe it. Let me see," Marcus demanded.

I pulled the piece of plastic out of my purse and handed it to him. He studied the permit for a few seconds and nodded his head. "Now if you could just learn how to drive, you'll be all right."

"I *can* drive," I said with attitude. "Tell him that I can drive, Daddy!"

Daddy was already on the porch, pushing his key into the lock of the front door. "She needs some work, but she'll be fine," he said. "She got us home safely, and that's what mattered most."

"See, I got us home safely," I said matter-of-factly, "and that's all that matters."

Marcus wrapped his arms around my waist and pulled me close. I inhaled his Kenneth Cole cologne—the fragrance that I'd bought him for Christmas. His lips gently brushed mine. "Congratulations," he whispered.

"Thanks," I whispered back.

Marcus—the guy of my dreams—had been my boyfriend for eleven months and twenty-six days. In less than a week, we would be celebrating our one-year anniversary. We were made for each other, despite the fact that we'd almost broken up over the summer. It had actually been my idea to make the stupid pact that we'd made—a pact to split up during our summer vacation, just in case one of us met someone new. We risked losing each other forever. Luckily, fate was on our side, and we'd ended up back in each other's arms by the end of the summer. No more pacts!

"I was headed to the mall. You want to come?" he asked. "Maybe we can check out a movie or something."

"Terrence isn't going?"

"Don't start, Indi."

"I'm just messing with you." I smiled. "Which mall?"

"Maybe Perimeter or Cumberland," he said.

"Cool. Let me just ask my parents if I can go." I jogged toward my front steps. "I'll be right back."

"You don't have time to change clothes and put on makeup and all that, Indi. Just ask and let's go."

It was as if he'd read my mind, because that was exactly what I had planned. I had already mentally picked out what I would wear—my new pair of jeans and my fuchsia top. I needed to do something different with my hair, tame it a little bit. I'd planned on freshening up and splashing on one of my Victoria's Secret fragrances. I also wanted to change out of my Chuck Taylor sneakers, which I'd worn to the DMV, and put on a pair of high-heeled boots. Marcus knew that I couldn't show up at the mall just any old way. You never knew who you might bump into. If we were just going to Stonecrest Mall, well, there would probably be no need to change clothes—what I had on would've been fine. I knew everybody who hung out there, anyway. But Perimeter Mall or Cumberland Mall—those were a different story. There would be lots of new faces, and good impressions were important. Marcus would just have to wait.

"I'm not playing, Indi. I'll leave you if you take too long," he threatened, even though he wasn't serious. If he left me, there would be hell to pay. He was always threatening to leave somebody. Especially on school mornings, if I took too long toasting my Pop-Tart, or if I spent too much time giggling with my girlfriends after dance-team practice. He was all bark and no bite.

"I'll be right back, Marcus. I promise."

It was a lie, and I knew it as I took two steps at a time, rushed inside and made a dash for the kitchen, where my mother was frying some chicken. Time was of the essence, but I had to do what I had to do. I grabbed a paper towel and stole a piece of chicken when my mother's back was turned.

"You're not slick, Indi. If you're gonna eat, sit down and fix a plate," she said.

"No time, Ma. I wanna go to the mall with Marcus," I said. "Can I?"

"You haven't cleaned up that room, Indigo. And I need you to fold those clothes that are in the dryer," she said. "I told you to do that last night, before you went to bed, and you haven't done it yet."

"Please, Mama. I promise I'll do it when I get back," I pleaded. "We won't be gone long."

"You better not be gone long, and I mean it." She was giving in. "You got stuff to do around here."

"I know. I promise I'll do it as soon as I get home." I kissed her cheek and then rushed upstairs.

★ ★ ★

As Marcus and I strolled past Bloomingdale's at Perimeter Mall, I was grateful that I'd changed into something more fly. I couldn't be outdressed by the girls who passed by and stared, with those envious looks in their eyes. I had to be able to fit right in, especially since they were also checking out my boyfriend.

"What are they looking at?" I had to ask as we passed by a group of girls who took turns staring at Marcus as if he were a piece of country-fried steak.

"Who?" Marcus asked, as if he was oblivious to all the attention.

"Those chicken heads that just passed by." I intertwined my fingers with his, just to let them know that we were together. "They were staring way too much."

"Hey, Marcus," one of them said, with a little too much sweetness in her voice, while the rest of them looked on.

"What's up?" he responded, all smiles.

What was he smiling at?

"Nice game on Friday night. You were good." She grinned, her lip gloss shining as she licked her lips in a sensual way. Her overdeveloped breasts were screaming from the tightness of her shirt—they wanted to be free. "I can't wait till we play your school again."

"I remember you," I interrupted. "You're that cheerleader who fell from the top of the pyramid at halftime. Are you okay?"

She had to be embarrassed. She'd fallen pretty hard, and there were sighs from everyone in the gymnasium as all eyes fell on her.

"I'm fine." She was annoyed that I had busted her out in front of Marcus.

"Good. 'Cause you fell pretty hard," I continued. I wanted to teach her a lesson about pushing up on somebody's man and acting as if I wasn't standing right there. With a little smirk on my face, I said, "I thought you were really hurt."

She rolled her eyes and led her posse away. "See you later, Marcus."

Marcus cut his eyes my way, with disapproval, of course.

"What?" I asked innocently.

"You a trip." He wrapped his arm around my neck, almost in a headlock, and we headed toward the movie theater. "You wanna check out a movie, or what?"

"Yes."

"You don't have to be jealous about other girls, you know."

"I wasn't jealous, Marcus. She just disrespected me."

"Disrespected you how?"

"Never mind. You wouldn't understand," I said. "You were too busy smiling."

"I'm just saying. You never have to worry about that. I'm yours, and you're mine," he said. "You're the only girl I want. Okay?"

"Okay." I smiled. I needed to hear that.

I wasn't really worried. The girl in question was no competition for me, but I had to always stand my ground—make my presence known. Otherwise, females would walk right over me, and that was unacceptable.

As Marcus handed me a tub of buttery popcorn, I kissed his cheek.

"I love you," I whispered.

There! I was the first to say it. So what? It was true. I did love Marcus. Although neither of us had ever verbalized it to the other, I felt a strong desire to tell Marcus what I was feeling for him…at that moment. Right there in the movie theater's concession-stand line. Then it hit me! *What if he doesn't feel the same? What if he doesn't love me back? What if he doesn't say it, too?*

"You want Coke or Dr. Pepper?" he asked, completely ignoring the fact that I'd just said *those three little words—those three little words,* which you never said to anyone unless you really meant them.

I wouldn't make a bigger fool of myself by confronting him, so I simply shrugged my shoulders and said, "Coke's fine."

I watched as the pimple-faced, redheaded boy behind the counter at the concession stand filled my cup with Coca-Cola. He handed it to me, and I immediately stuck a straw in the cup. Marcus took a long drink from his Sprite and wrapped his arm around my neck as we entered the dark auditorium. We found a couple of empty seats, and Marcus plopped down beside me, handed me the huge carton of popcorn and opened his box of Milk Duds. I stuffed buttery popcorn into my mouth and stared at the screen as the action-packed previews began to play.

I wished I hadn't spilled my guts to Marcus. Wished I hadn't been the first to say "I love you," but what was done was done. You can't take back words once you've said them, and besides, it was the truth. I did love Marcus. I loved everything about him—his smile, the way he threw Skittles or M&M's at my bedroom window to wake me up in the morning. I loved how he treated me and how he tutored me in math, even though I gave him a hard time. He cared if I succeeded, and he had manners—which my parents also loved. He did little things, like slip Little Debbie cupcakes into my backpack or send me text messages just to say hi. He listened to me when I vented about Miss Martin and the dance team and encouraged me not to give up.

Suddenly, his fingers intertwined with mine, and we watched the movie in silence.

After the movie, I was quiet in Marcus's Jeep as we took I-285 back to College Park. He slipped a Lil Wayne CD in, and rap music filled the Jeep. As Marcus pulled up in front of his house, I was the first to hop out. I stood next to the curb, my hands stuffed into the pockets of my coat.

"I'll see you tomorrow, Marcus, sometime after church," I said.

Marcus headed around to my side of the Jeep, hugged me.

"Cool," he said. "Send me a text before you go to sleep."

I headed toward my porch, and Marcus headed toward his. With his hood on his head, he said, "Hey, Indi."

I turned around. "Yeah?"

"I love you, too." He smiled.

Took him long enough, I thought as I smiled, too. I was worried there for a minute, but Marcus took all of my cares away with those little words.

No other words were spoken. I just stepped inside my warm house, leaned against the front door after it was shut. My heart did a little dance.

five

Tameka

WITH short pleated skirts on our hips and pom-poms on our fists, we strutted out to the center of the floor—Indigo on one side of me and Jade on the other. It was a routine that we'd created ourselves—every move, every swing of the hips, every sway of the arms had been strategically designed for us by us. Miss Martin had split the entire team up into groups of three and challenged each group to come up with their own routine, and the team with the best routine would have the privilege of performing it at a real game, during halftime. It was a challenge that Indigo, Jade and I welcomed. After all, we were the three best dancers on the entire junior varsity team, anyway. It was no surprise that our group won the challenge, and it was our routine that would be performed during halftime for the entire student body and their mamas.

As Usher's track bounced against the gymnasium walls, we swayed to the music. The crowd was into it, standing in the bleachers and clapping their hands. I saw my mother's face among the other faces in the bleachers; there was a huge smile on hers. She usually came to every football and basketball game throughout the season, wearing the school's colors and showing more pep than any of the other parents. She was standing and clapping, and when she moved to the left a little bit I noticed that my daddy was in the bleachers, too, sitting right next to her. He never showed up at our games and had never even seen me perform before. But he was there that night and was even wearing the school's colors.

Knowing Daddy was in the bleachers gave me energy. I barely got to spend any time with him, because he was always working, but he'd promised to try and make it to the game. I'd told him about the competition, and how Indigo, Jade and I had won the challenge. I had even showed him the routine. I was hopeful, but not convinced, that he would be there. I was surprised to see his face in the crowd.

Daddy was reserved and very laid-back, which was why he wasn't standing and yelling my name across the gymnasium like Mommy was. She was the exact opposite of him. She wasn't reserved at all. In fact, I used to wonder what had drawn the two of them together in the first place, because they were nothing alike. I guess that proved that opposites really did attract. It was sort of like Vance and me. We were different. I loved to dance, and he stumbled over his feet when he even tried. He made exceptional grades in school; mine were mediocre. Both of Vance's parents were professionals: his mother was an attorney and his father a dentist. Although my father was a music producer, my mother stayed at home, cooked and cleaned house. His parents were big on education—there were no other options for Vance besides college. My mother never graduated from high school. Instead, she got her GED much later in life. My parents wanted me to go to college, but if I didn't, it wouldn't be the end of the world. They just wanted me to be successful at whatever I chose. Vance's father would probably disown him if he didn't attend Duke University. I guess, in a sense, we were opposites, too.

Daddy blew me a kiss as I took a bow at the end of my routine and rushed off the floor.

From the sidelines, I watched as Vance and the other basketball players rushed out onto the floor. Terrence Hill took the ball out of bounds and passed it to Marcus Carter. Marcus passed it to Vance, who set up the play for the team and took it down court. I watched as he dribbled the ball, his muscular legs showing beneath his shorts. He had a fresh haircut, and his chocolate-brown face was pimple free. The gold bracelet that I'd given him for Christmas was dangling from his wrist with every bounce of the ball, and when he licked his lips, he looked just like LL Cool J.

At the end of the game, with twelve seconds left on the clock, Jaylen Thomas sent the basketball floating through the air. The ball bounced off the rim and into the hands of the other team. Lenny Jackson, from the other team, rushed to the other end of the court, and their cheerleaders went crazy as he sunk the ball into the basket. The score changed, and they were ahead by two points. With two seconds left on the clock, it was over. We'd lost, and everybody knew it. Any chance of coming back was a long shot. Vance and his teammates hung their heads while the other team's members jumped for joy, slapping high fives with one another as the buzzer sounded across the gym.

If only we could get those twelve seconds back, and someone other than Jaylen Thomas would've attempted the shot—either Marcus or Terrence, who were much better ballplayers. Jaylen was better at defense and had had no business with the ball at such a critical time in the game. Couldn't he have just played defense and left the three-pointers to someone who knew how to shoot the ball?

The basketball team made their way to the locker room, their heads hung low. Coach Hardy followed behind with his clip-board in hand, a wrinkle in the center of his forehead—the one he always got when our team lost. I gave Vance a half smile as he passed by. He didn't smile back, just raised his eyebrows. He was disappointed. Nobody wanted to lose.

"I'll meet you right here after you change, okay?" I said.

"Yeah," he mumbled.

Indigo hugged Marcus, and he kissed her forehead. "Go, Tigers!" she said, showing support for the team even though they'd lost.

"Go, Tigers!" Jade said.

"Go, Tigers!" I said, and before long the entire dance team began to chant.

"Go, Tigers!" We all said it over and over again, trying our best to make them feel better.

Soon some of their frowns became smiles.

Outside after the game, I stood at the curb, next to my parents' SUV, zipped my coat and threw a black toboggan on my head.

"Can I hang out with the rest of the team?" I asked.

"Hang out where?" Mommy asked.

"We're just going to McDonald's," I said as Indi stood nearby. "Indi's dad will bring me home."

"Harold's gonna pick y'all up from McDonald's, Indi?" Mommy asked as if I was lying.

"Yes, ma'am," Indigo answered.

"What time?" Daddy asked.

"He just said for us to call when we're ready," Indigo said. "Shouldn't be much later than eleven-thirty or twelve, though."

"Okay, that should be fine," Mommy said as she opened the door of the SUV and hopped inside to shield herself from the brisk Atlanta wind. "Come on. Let's go, Paul. It's cold out here. If they're just going to Mickey D's, she'll be all right. And I trust Harold to bring her home."

"Thanks." I kissed my mother's cheek and waved to my daddy.

I watched as they pulled away from the curb and waited just long enough before rushing to find Vance's old 280z in the school's parking lot. He had the engine running, and his hoodie was zipped all the way up to his neck. I hopped into the passenger seat of the car.

"Hey," I said.

"Hey." He said it with very little enthusiasm. "Your parents okay with us hanging out?"

"I told them that I was hanging with Indi. When I hang out with you, there are too many rules and red tape, so I figured it was easier this way. But it's cool. We'll all be hanging out together at McDonald's, right?"

"Eventually. But first I gotta stop by my house right quick. Gotta let Jinx out and feed him." He pulled out of the school's parking lot. "My parents are out of town, and there's nobody else there to feed and walk him."

Jinx was Vance's Doberman, a dog that I often heard barking in the background when we talked on the phone. I'd never had a desire to meet Jinx in person, though. I wasn't really an animal person.

"Okay," I said. How long could it take to let a dog out to pee and to fix him a bowl of dog chow?

We pulled into Vance's subdivision; rows of beautiful houses stood tall with their manicured lawns. Vance's family lived in one of the more expensive neighborhoods in College Park, the kind that had a security gate. He hit the garage-door opener attached to his sun visor, and we pulled into the three-car garage. Jinx rushed toward the passenger door, and I sat still, my heart pounding fast. Vance stepped out of the car.

"Jinx, come here!" he yelled and then snapped a leash on his collar. "It's okay, Tameka. You can get out. He won't mess with you."

I slowly opened my door and walked to the back of the car

as Vance took Jinx outside, near the curb. Jinx was playful and jumped around like a little kid before finally lifting his leg and relieving himself.

"Go inside that door," Vance told me before bringing Jinx back into the garage.

I stepped inside the door and into a huge kitchen with shiny hardwood floors. The silver refrigerator was bigger than any I'd ever seen. With lots of cabinets, it had to be the biggest kitchen I'd ever seen, too. It looked like one of those kitchens that you saw on HGTV or on *MTV Cribs*. I adjusted the strap of my Coach purse on my shoulder and stood in the middle of the kitchen floor, waiting for Vance.

"Relax," he whispered in my ear from behind. I hadn't even heard him walk into the room.

He removed my purse from my arm and placed it on the kitchen counter, grabbed my hand and led me up a flight of stairs right off the kitchen. It was like one of those hidden stairways, like the one on *The Cosby Show* reruns.

"Where are we going?" I asked.

"I wanna show you around," he said.

We took a stroll down the long hallway, my Nike sneakers making a squishing noise with every step. We stepped into the huge master bedroom, which looked like a mini apartment. It had a sofa, a huge flat-screen television hung from the wall, and the built-in bookshelf probably had a thousand books.

"This is my mom and dad's room," he said. "Big, huh?"

"That's not even the word," I said, looking around until my eyes landed on the huge bookcase. "I can see that somebody likes to read."

"My mother is an avid reader. She reads, like, five books a week." He laughed. "Come on. I wanna show you my crib."

I followed Vance down the long stretch of the hallway and into a room that was smaller than his parents' bedroom, but not much. The entertainment center against the wall held Vance's flat-screen television, a DVD player, stereo equipment and lots of other electronic gadgets. The comforter on his king-size bed was a tribute to the New York Jets, and posters of LeBron James, Kobe Bryant and Dwyane Wade were plastered all over the walls. He hit the power button on his stereo, and Keyshia Cole's voice rang throughout the room.

"You okay?" He hopped onto his bed.

"Yeah."

"Have a seat," he said and patted the spot next to him on the bed. "I won't bite."

I sat next to Vance, and before I could relax, his arms were pulling me closer. His lips touched mine, and I remembered all those dreams I'd had about kissing him. Only this time it was for real, and I decided to savor the moment. His fingertips began to caress my breasts, and at first, I wanted to pull away, but I relaxed against his touch. He stretched out across the bed, on his back, and pulled me on top of him. As soon as he began to pull down the zipper of my skinny jeans, I felt uncomfortable. I remembered our conversation the other night, the one that had left me sleepless until four o'clock in the morning. I wanted to be in Vance's arms, but it was happening too fast. Sex was like being on a roller-coaster ride at Six Flags Over Georgia—once you were on it, there was no getting off. This was unknown territory for Vance and me, and I wasn't sure I was ready for it.

I pulled away and sat straight up on the edge of the bed.

"What's up?" Vance asked, breathing heavily.

"I'm not ready for this," I said.

"I thought you said you'd done it before," he said. "Not scared, are you?"

"A little," I admitted.

"I got you. I promise I won't hurt you," Vance whispered.

I had never seen this side of him before. Up until then, he'd been somewhat of a quiet guy, smart, with future goals and dreams. But today he was a teenage boy, with hormones raging out of control. It was confusing and a little scary.

"I'm not ready. I think this is something we should talk about first and make sure it's the right time."

"I tried to talk to you about it the other night, remember?" Of course I remembered. "Everybody's doing it, Tameka," he said, and then his lips touched mine again. "And it's the perfect time. My folks are gone, and we have the whole house to ourselves. And…I got protection, if that's what you're worried about." He reached into the drawer of his nightstand, pulled out three or four condoms and placed them near the lamp.

"I need to get over to Mickey D's. That's where I told my parents I would be. I wanna be there when Mr. Summer picks up Indigo so he can take me home, too. My parents trust me to be responsible, and I don't want to mess that up."

"You think making love to your boyfriend is irresponsible?" he asked. "I have girls throwing it at me on a daily basis, Tameka, but really I just want it to be with you."

"Girls like who?" All I heard was the word *girls*. I wanted to know who these girls were, and if he was catching it when they were throwing it at him.

"Like, a bunch of girls. I don't keep track." He stood, grabbed the autographed football from his bookshelf, tossed it into the air.

I was flooded with jealousy at the thought of other girls pushing up on Vance. At that moment I was faced with a decision—the decision to give it up simply because that was what I was expected to do. Or walk away, think it through and not make a hasty decision. I thought about my mother and how she had taught me to never let anyone touch my "pocketbook" before I was ready. I could still hear her voice in my head, giving me the same lecture that she'd given me a million times.

"Please take me to McDonald's, where the rest of my friends are, so I can catch a ride home."

Vance pulled his car keys from the pocket of his jeans, held them in the air. "Let's go," he said.

In the car, he turned on V-103's Quiet Storm.

"You mad?" I asked.

"Nah, I'm cool," he said. "You cool?"

"I'm okay."

"I didn't mean to rush you into something you weren't ready for, Tameka. I'm sorry." He sounded so sincere.

Now that was the Vance I knew—sweet, respectful. His fingertips brushed against my cheek.

"Thank you for understanding." I smiled.

He shrugged.

I could see the golden arches up ahead, and I wondered if I'd made the right decision. After all, we were in a serious relationship. Not just a fly-by-night, casual sort of thing. We'd made vows and promises. I just wondered what was required in a serious relationship. Did you give up your right to say no? Not to mention, girls were throwing it at him on a daily basis. It was just a matter of time before he considered going somewhere else, and I knew it.

"Just let me know when you're ready," he said.

I buttoned my coat up, slipped my gloves onto my hands, pulled my toboggan onto my head and braced myself for the night air.

SIX

Vance

I listened to the score on ESPN as my eyes slowly drifted shut. I hit the mute button on the television and hit the power button for the stereo. Lil Wayne spit some lyrics to me on 107.9. Things with Tameka hadn't gone as planned. She wanted to wait until we had talked about having sex before we actually did it. What sense did that make? *What a waste of an empty house,* I thought as my head bounced against my pillow, and I struggled to stay awake and catch the score from the game.

My phone vibrated on my nightstand. I picked it up. A text from Tameka.

WUP?

Nuthin, I typed.

Just wanted 2 say GNITE.

U OK?

Yes.

Cool.

CUIMD, she typed. It was her favorite phrase. See you in my dreams.

:-O I gave her a yawn to let her know that I was sleepy.

GNITE, she responded, and then she was gone.

I kicked my sneakers off and heard them hit the floor with a loud thud. I pulled my shirt over my head and removed my jeans. I was down to my boxers and tube socks. I thought I heard a noise, like someone was in the house, even though I knew I had locked up. I decided to go downstairs and check the doors, make sure the house was secured. I peeked into the garage just to make sure I'd let the garage door down when I came in. I checked the front door, made sure it was locked. Checked the back door. All locks were secured. I swung open the refrigerator door, hoping for a late-night snack. I searched the freezer and ended up with an ice-cream sandwich and a bottle of Gatorade. I took the stairs two at a time to my room, plopped onto the bed. My phone vibrated again. Maybe Tameka had had a change of heart and was planning to sneak out of the house and head back over here for a nightcap—that way we could finish what we'd started earlier.

I picked up my phone. Read the text.

Hi U.

It wasn't from Tameka, and I didn't recognize the phone number.

Who is this?

Guess.

Someone wanted to play games, and I wasn't in the mood. It was too late at night, and I wasn't in the best of moods, anyway, after losing to the worst team in the district. Not only had we lost our game against a team that sucked, but on top of it, I had issues with my girl, too.

Not in da mood 4 games.

It's Darla. From Am Hist.

Darla from American history? The fine girl with the cute little dimples?

How did u get my #? I wanted to know. I didn't remember giving it to her.

Got my sources :)

Girls had a way of tracking you down, no matter what. The more you tried to avoid someone, the more they chased. However, with Darla, I didn't mind the chase.

WUP? I asked.

U looked good on da court 2Nite.

U were there?

Yes.

Cool.

U got a G-fnd, huh?

Yep.

Serious?

Somewhat.

Cool. Let's B friends.

Sounds good.

CU L8R.

L8R.

She was gone, but thoughts of her still danced in my head. So much so that I wasn't even sleepy anymore. I wanted to text her again but didn't. I hoped that she would text me back, but she didn't. It was better that way. I had a girl, and Darla was way too cute for her own good. She would have me distracted, and I didn't need that right now.

I closed my eyes really tight and hoped for sleep.

Saturday morning, and I had a laundry list of chores. Cleaning the guest bathroom was at the top of that list, along with mopping the kitchen floor and vacuuming the family room. My parents were sticklers for a clean house, and they didn't hire anyone to do it. My mother cleaned like a mad-woman, and they depended on my sister, Lori, and me to do our part. And since Lori ended up going to Philadelphia with them to visit my grandmother, she weaseled out of her chores.

In my opinion, because she was twelve years old, she was able weasel out of a lot of things.

It simply wasn't fair that she had the bigger bedroom, a bigger television and a huge closet to hold all her clothes, which she received for absolutely no reason whatsoever. If she aced a math quiz, she got a new outfit. When she made the volleyball team at her school, she got a new Nintendo Wii system, with four new games. I made good grades on a daily basis, and I was the starting guard for the school's basketball team, but I didn't have a Nintendo Wii. I was still using the PlayStation I'd got two Christmases before, and the joystick barely worked, depending on what day it was. My sister was truly rotten and got on my nerves just for the heck of it. If it had been up to me, I would've been an only child. Instead, I was stuck with her for at least the rest of my life.

I wiped down the toilet in the guest bathroom, poured a little Pine-Sol into the bowl in order to make the room smell fresh and clean. After vacuuming the family room, I collapsed onto the leather sofa, placed my feet on top of the coffee table. That was a no-no when my parents were home—feet on the furniture was absolutely out of the question. But what my parents didn't know wouldn't hurt them. They were way too involved in my decision making, anyway; my dad was, at least. Especially when it came to my college choice. I knew what I wanted and was mature enough to make my own decisions, but trying to get him to see that was like pulling teeth.

When my phone vibrated, I jumped. Looked at the screen. Jaylen.

"What up, fool?" I answered.

"We going to the mall?" he asked.

"For sho."

"You picking me up?" he asked.

"Um, I'll think about it," I teased.

"I'll be ready when you get here," he said and hung up before I could object.

Jaylen was my best friend. We played ball together and hung out most other times. We'd been tighter than glue since the first grade. The girls loved his six-foot frame, light brown skin and good hair. He was broke most of the time, though, and borrowed lunch money from me on a regular basis. That was what kept him from keeping a regular girlfriend. Girls expected you to take them to a movie or to McDonald's once in a while. You couldn't do that if you were always broke.

I put the cleaning products away and then rushed upstairs to take a shower. I was hungry but decided I'd grab something at the food court at the mall. I listened to *SportsCenter* as I sat on the edge of the bed and tied my green-and-white Nike sneakers. I decided on my Southpole jeans and my green-and-white Southpole shirt. I brushed my hair until the waves appeared, and got upset when I saw a pimple growing on my light brown forehead. It was all I needed.

The minute that Jaylen hopped into my car, he took over my stereo.

"You gotta hear this track that we put down last night," he declared.

Music was his life. It was all he thought about. He had a makeshift studio in his basement, where we spent hours recording and putting lyrics to beats. Sometimes on the weekends, we recorded until the wee hours of the morning. We had enough music to drop a demo. We were good, both of us could flow, but the problem was getting someone to listen. That was why I hoped for a chance meeting with Tameka's father. He had a lot of pull in the music industry, and I knew that if he ever heard our stuff, he would be impressed.

As the music filled the car, I smiled. It sounded good.

"Where'd you get that beat?" I asked.

"You'll never believe it." He grinned. "You know Terrence Hill from the basketball team, right? Well, his little brother, Trey...I think he's, like, ten years old or something... He creates beats...."

"Come on, man. A ten-year-old created this beat?" I asked.

I wanted to meet this musical genius. I didn't know Terrence that well, but he seemed cool. I guessed he would be our go-to man from now on, whenever we needed a hot track.

"I kid you not," Jaylen said. "Get it? *Kid* you not."

Jaylen had the corniest sense of humor of anybody that I knew. He wasn't the most popular dude at school, but he was cool. He was more like family to me, because we'd known each other for so long. We'd grown up on the playground of our elementary school together, skinned our knees together, and both of us had lost our two front teeth in the same week.

The beat was hot, the lyrics were hot, and we bounced our heads to the music all the way down I-287.

seven

Tameka

The relaxer was cold against my scalp, and it didn't take long for it to begin to sting. I bit my bottom lip in order to ease the pain. It was no secret, I was tender headed. Cynthia knew it, and she usually took extra care in making my beauty-shop experience as painless as possible.

"You burning, sweetie?" she asked as she slapped the rat-tailed comb against my scalp.

"A little bit." I frowned.

"Just a few more minutes and then we'll wash it out," Cynthia said. Her hair was in a red Afro, and low-cut jeans hugged her hips. "How you doing over there, Mel?"

"I think I'm dry," my mother said.

"Meka, you go on over to the shampoo bowl. Mel, you can have a seat right here in my chair."

Saturday mornings at the beauty shop took up half of our day, but it was always worth it, because we looked so fly when Cynthia finally finished working her magic on us. It was cool sitting there listening to all the latest adult gossip. I always learned something new—grown-ups were a trip.

I leaned my head back against the shampoo bowl and Cynthia washed the relaxer out of my hair. The smell of the shampoo that she'd used to wash my hair filled the room, made my scalp tingle. Cynthia was running her mouth nonstop with the heavy woman who sat under the dryer across the room. They talked about what was on sale at Dillard's, traffic and Cynthia's latest trip to Las Vegas. She had won two thousand dollars at the slot machines but then lost it all before she left. But she'd had the time of her life.

Cynthia wrapped my hair and then sat me under the dryer. I flipped through an *Essence* magazine and read a few of the articles. After getting bored with that, I flipped open my cell phone, decided to send Vance a text message. The night before had left us both feeling awkward, but I hoped we could get past it.

Hey U. I sent a quick message, waited for the reply.

There was none. I figured he'd probably slept in, as he did most Saturday mornings. The heat from the hair dryer made me doze.

"Okay, let's go, Meka." Cynthia woke me up with a tap on the shoulder. "Go sit in my chair."

I opened my eyes and glanced across the room at my mother, or at least at the woman I thought was my mother. The woman favored her, all the way down to the tight-fitting red Guess shirt and the skinny jeans. The only difference was this woman had a short, sassy haircut, and my mother wore her hair thick and shoulder-length.

"How do you like it?" this woman asked, staring straight at me.

"What did you do?" I asked.

"I told you I was cutting it all off."

She really was my mother, only she'd lost her mind.

"That is so cute," said the skinny woman who'd just hopped from Cynthia's chair. She grinned from ear to ear. "I want my hair just like that, Cyn."

All eyes were on Mom and her new short haircut. It *was* cute, but I couldn't believe she'd just cut all her hair off, like a crazy woman. My daddy was going to flip out. The more I looked, though, the more I liked it.

"Do you like it, Tameka?" my mother asked.

"It's cool," I said. "Looks good on you."

My mother was a brand-new woman.

It was well into the afternoon, and I still hadn't heard from Vance. I opened my phone and stared at the blank screen. Decided to send him another text message.

Where R U? I asked.

No reply. Not right away.

At da mall, was his response ten minutes later.

Buyin me something? I teased.

What U want? he asked.

Pretzel & smoothie, I said.

Those were our two favorite things at the mall—a hot pretzel dipped in mustard from the pretzel shop next to Dillard's and a peach-mango smoothie, which we usually shared. Vance usually drank more than his share of the smoothie, leaving me with about one-fourth. But I didn't care. It was our thing. The more I thought about it, the more I missed Vance. I had replayed the night before a million times in my head. What if I had given in to Vance? Maybe I wouldn't feel so distant.

Peach mango? he asked.

Yep.

You got it. I could almost hear his smile.

We were okay. He wasn't mad, after all, and that was enough for me.

Cynthia styled my hair in a cute flat-ironed look. The usual. Unlike my mother, I was afraid to try new things. It was always safest to go with the usual. I wished I could be more like her— confident, self-assured. Instead, I questioned my every thought, and every decision was calculated. It was rare that I just did something out of the ordinary. I was too worried about what people would think if I failed.

In the car, I tuned the radio to 107.9, and the voice of the Saturday-morning disc jockey Mizz Shyneka rang out across the airways. After she gave her little spiel, she spun a track, and Mommy and I bounced to the music. Hip-hop was something that we both had in common. We traded CDs like best friends did, and if I couldn't find one of my CDs, she was usually the culprit. I'd usually find it in the CD player in her car, or in her bedroom.

"You want a chicken sandwich from Chik-fil-A?" she asked. "I'm kinda hungry."

"I could use some chicken nuggets," I told her.

"Your hair looks fabulous." She smiled as she pulled into Chik-fil-A's drive-through.

"Look at you, with a short haircut!" I laughed. "What is really going on? You got a new boyfriend or something?"

"I just needed a change." She ran her fingers through her short locks. "Maybe Daddy will pay more attention...."

She seemed serious when she made that comment. I knew that my father's absence from home and the fact that he was a workaholic bothered her more than she let on.

"He does pay attention, Mommy."

"Yeah, when he's home," she said sarcastically. "I just wonder how much time he actually spends working."

"Are you serious?" I asked. She sounded insecure. "Do you think he's doing something, you know, wrong?"

"I just think he spends too much time away from home. That's all." She forced a smile and changed the subject. "What are you having with those nuggets, sweetie?"

"Um, um, just some curly fries and a Coke."

I was thrown off by her comments. It almost sounded as if she thought he was having an affair. Suddenly it dawned on me.

What if he was? Would he leave us for someone else? Would they get a divorce like my friend Jade's parents had? She had talked about how terrible it was when her mother moved them to New Jersey after her parents were divorced. And even though they'd moved back to Atlanta, her parents never got back together. Instead, her father ended up marrying someone else. That would be a nightmare. I couldn't think about that. Mommy was just being silly. Daddy would never leave us.

Once in my room, I hit the play button on my stereo. Rihanna's voice rang through the room. I fell backward onto my bed and listened to the music. Wished this were a different Saturday. On a different Saturday, Vance would've sent me a text as soon as his feet hit the floor. He would've invited me to the mall. It was then that it hit me—maybe he was at the mall with someone else, sharing a pretzel and a peach-mango smoothie with her. I needed to know for sure, and there was only one way to find out.

"Mom," I yelled as I rushed downstairs to the kitchen, where she was loading dishes into the dishwasher, "can you take me to the mall?"

"I can drop you off and pick you up later on. I have a book-club meeting this afternoon," she said. "Are you going by yourself?"

"I think Indi and the other girls are already there. I wanna try and catch up with them," I told her.

"Are you ready now?" she asked.

"Let me just grab my purse."

I rushed upstairs, grabbed my Coach purse and placed some eyeliner on my eyes and lip gloss on my lips. I checked my jeans out in the mirror and thought they looked okay. I slipped my Nike's off and placed my Coach-designed Chuck Taylors on my feet. They were beige and brown and matched my Coach purse. I grabbed sixty dollars out of my stash from my jewelry box with the ballerina on top. The jewelry box had been a gift from Daddy when I was five years old. He knew even back then that I would be a dancer.

Daddy had an eye for talent. As a music producer, he was in the business of deciding who had talent and who didn't. And his job was an important one; Mommy and I had always known that. She had always been his biggest supporter, but our conversation at Chik-fil-A had me doubting the strength of that support. I needed to know what our future held.

After dropping me off in front of Macy's, I watched as Mommy drove away. I was glad she had her book-club sisters to keep her company while I hung out at the mall. I checked my purse to make sure my cell phone was inside, pulled it out and called Indigo. There was no answer. I could've sworn they'd said they were going to the mall. I sent her a text message and then stepped inside Macy's.

eight

Vance

I popped into Foot Locker, checked out the new Jordans. They were on sale, but not quite my price yet. I told the salesman to bring me a size eleven anyway. I slipped them onto my feet. Perfect fit. As I checked them out in the mirror, I decided that they were a must-have, regardless of the price.

"I'll take these, my man," I said.

As I approached the counter, I pulled my wallet out and checked my cash. I had about forty dollars. Not quite enough to cover the $149 price tag that the Jordans had on them. I pulled my credit card out of its little slot—the credit card that my parents had given me for emergencies.

This is strictly for emergencies, Vance. I could hear my dad's voice in my head. *This is not to be used on foolishness.*

I hesitated for a moment. I knew that the card was only to be used in case I ran out of gas and was stranded on the side of the road, or if my tire had a blowout. I knew what my father meant by *emergency.* But in my opinion, this *was* an emergency, in every sense of the word. The price on these Jordans wouldn't last forever. Not to mention, nobody—and I mean nobody—had a pair of shoes like this at my school.

The price, including tax, flashed across the screen on the cash register in bright green digital numbers. I handed the salesman my Visa. He swiped it and handed it back. It was a done deal when he handed over my receipt. The transaction had been made, and the Jordans were mine, regardless of the consequences. There was a chance that my dad would just pay the bill and not even look at the charges. It would be all right.

"What you get?" Jaylen asked as I stepped out of the store.

"Got the new Jordans." I grinned, proud of my purchase. "Ain't nobody got these."

"Let me see," he insisted.

"Naw, man, you'll see when I bust out in them on Monday morning," I said. "You'll see 'em then."

"There's some hotties hanging out over there by the movie theater. Let's go holler at a few of them." Jaylen changed the subject.

"Man, I don't feel like being bothered with chicken heads today," I said. "Let's go over to Dave & Buster's and shoot some pool."

"You gotta pay at Dave and Buster's and I only got, like, five bucks."

"Man, you always broke." I laughed. "How you expect to holler at some hotties?"

"Shut up, man."

We strolled through the mall, stopping to grab a burger at Wendy's. While standing in the long line, I felt a light tap on my arm and turned to find the most beautiful pair of brown eyes looking at me.

"Hey, Vance," Darla purred.

Two girls that I didn't recognize stood beside her. One looked like she could've been her twin sister; she had the same sexy body and cute smile. The other one looked like she'd eaten one pork chop too many. The three of them stood there, with their hands on their hips.

"What's up?" I asked Darla.

"What you doing here?" she asked.

What did most people do at the mall? Shop!

"Just hanging out," I said.

"You going to see that new Tyler Perry movie? It's playing now." She smiled. "That's where we're going."

"You should come," Darla's look-alike said.

"Um…" Jaylen cleared his throat and reached his hand out to Darla's look-alike. "I'm Jaylen. My boy here is rude."

"My bad," I said. "Darla, this is Jaylen. Jaylen, Darla."

"This is my cousin, Alexis," Darla said, introducing her look-alike.

"What's up?" I said to Alexis.

"And this is my friend Nita." Darla introduced the heavy girl, who was licking her lips at Jaylen.

"You going to the movies?" Nita asked Jaylen. "I'll buy you some popcorn."

Popcorn was the last thing she needed, I thought as I checked her out. She had a cute face, but her body didn't seem to match.

"I'm good. Thanks, though." Jaylen smiled and then focused all of his attention on Alexis. Even with Jaylen's six-foot frame and perfect haircut, Alexis seemed uninterested in him. But that didn't stop him from trying to get her attention.

Regardless of the fact that we both had girlfriends, we still found ourselves standing in the long, endless line at the movie theater. It wasn't a date. That was what I told myself as we got closer to the box office to purchase tickets. It was just a group of friends checking out a movie together. That was it. A date was more a one-on-one thing. If I was on a date with Darla,

I'd have my arm around her neck, and I would plant kisses on her forehead. If this were a date, I'd be buying her ticket to the movie. But I'd already decided that I was only buying mine. And maybe Jaylen's, because he was broke as a joke.

I slipped Jaylen one of the twenties from my wallet, just so he wouldn't be embarrassed in front of the girls. There was nothing worse than standing in a long line at the movies and getting to the box office and not being able to pay for your own ticket. As Jaylen approached the ticket counter, he turned and smiled at Alexis.

"Two student tickets," he said to the pimple-faced girl behind the counter. "I got you, Lex."

I got you, Lex? What was he doing? Did he forget that he was spending my twenty?

"Thank you," Alexis said and smiled.

Her whole attitude toward Jaylen changed after he spent some money on her. Girls.

Darla's beautiful brown eyes were staring straight at me. She didn't say it, but I knew she expected me to spring for her ticket. Jaylen had me in a bind, and I would let him know it as soon as we were alone. I wanted to pop him upside his head, but instead, I gave Darla a smile and handed the cashier my last twenty-dollar bill.

"Two students, please," I told Pimple Face.

I wasn't paying for her fat friend, I thought as I handed over the twenty. She must've figured that out, because she pulled her wallet out of her purse and paid for her own ticket.

As the five of us headed toward the concession stand, I spotted Tameka's friend Indigo Summer. She was with Jade Morgan and two other girls from the dance team, Tymia and Asia. All I needed was for them to spot me. One of them would be on the phone with Tameka quicker than I could explain why I was standing next to a beautiful girl in the concession-stand line at the movie theater. Not to mention, a girl that Tameka had already had words with. I didn't need that kind of drama.

"Hey, I'm going to the bathroom," I told them. I needed an exit strategy.

As I headed toward the men's room, Indigo spotted me.

"Hey, Vance. Who you here with?" she asked. "Tameka with you?"

"Nah, I'm here with that knuckleheaded Jaylen," I explained. It wasn't totally a lie. I *was* with Jaylen. "We're going to see that action-packed, um, movie."

"Which one?" Jade asked, all up in a conversation that didn't involve her.

"Did y'all see Tyler Perry's movie?" I asked, avoiding Jade's question.

"Yes, and it was so good," Indigo said. "You'll have to bring Tameka to see it. We invited her to come along, but she had to go get her hair done today. She will love this movie! It's my second time seeing it. Marcus brought me the first time."

"Who're those girls over there with Jaylen?" Jade interrupted again.

"Pssst." I blew air from my lips. "You know how Jaylen is. He's a girl magnet. I can't take him nowhere. I don't even know who he's over there talking to."

"Isn't he dating Kendra Thompson?" Asia asked.

"I'm not sure anymore," I lied. "Last I heard, they were on the rocks."

"For real?" Tymia asked, her hands on her small hips. "Because she was just bragging about him, like, two days ago. Talking about how they were all in love. She would die if she saw him now, cheesing all up in that girl's face like that."

"That looks like Darla Union over there," Jade added. "She's the new girl in my algebra class. I loaned her a pencil the other day."

"She's also the one that Tameka almost beat down after practice the other day," Asia said. "She got a smart mouth. That's all I can say."

"Yeah, they got into it over something silly," Indigo said. "She seems like a nice person, though. I think it was just a misunderstanding on Tameka's part."

"She told me she was a cheerleader at her other school," Tymia said.

The conversation was becoming way too uncomfortable. Too much talk about this girl—Darla Union. It was making me nervous, and I needed to escape.

"Hey, I gotta go to the restroom. I'ma holler at y'all." I started dancing around like I really had to go.

"Okay, Vance. We'll talk to you later," Indigo said.

"We'll tell Tameka that we saw you," Jade added, with that look on her face. A look that said, I know what you're up to.

Before they could say another word, I disappeared into the restroom. It felt safe there. I wasn't really cheating on Tameka, although it felt like I was. I just needed to make it through this movie, and the rest would be history.

nine

Tameka

I filled my black shopping basket with three bottles of shower gel and three bottles of lotion. I grabbed four pairs of sexy underwear and a pair of sleep pants. I smelled the new fragrances as I waited for Indigo and the other girls to meet me at Victoria's Secret. Indigo had finally replied to my text message and had said that they were just leaving the movie theater. I was glad they were still at the mall when my mom dropped me off, because I'd needed to get out of the house something terrible.

"Ooh, your hair is cute!" Indigo said as she stepped into Victoria's Secret, wearing the leather jacket that her parents had bought her for Christmas.

"What's up, Tameka?" Tymia said.

"You got all kinds of stuff in this bag. You look like you're shopping for groceries." Jade laughed.

"It's just a few things." I smiled.

"You missed the movie. It was so good." Asia touched my hair and got a closer look at it. "Your hair looks so silky and shiny. What kinda relaxer does your stylist use?"

"I'm not sure. I just sit in her chair and let her do her thing," I said.

"We saw Vance," Jade announced. "He was at the movies."

"With who?" I asked, with attitude, my hands on my hips. I remembered I hadn't heard from him all day.

"With his bigheaded friend Jaylen," Indigo said.

"And some girls," Jade added.

"Those girls weren't with them. Why you tryin' to start something?" Indigo asked. "Jaylen was just standing in the concession-stand line, talking to some girls from school."

"What girls?" I asked. My heart was beating fast. I was afraid of what I might hear next, but I wanted all the details.

"Darla Union," Jade said. "You know, the one you were about to beat down the other day? She was with a few other girls. I don't know if they were all together, though. But it looked like it."

"Personally, I don't think they were together," Indigo said.

"Maybe you should just call and ask him," Tymia suggested. "Or better yet, let's just go see if the movie let out yet."

"Yeah, let's do that," I said.

After paying for my loot, I followed as Jade led the way to the movie theater. Was Vance with another girl, or was I just feeling insecure all of a sudden? I pulled my cell phone out of my purse, dialed Vance's phone number. It didn't even ring before I heard his deep voice saying, "Sorry I can't answer my phone right now, but leave me a message, and I'll hit you back." Lil Wayne's voice sang in the background before I heard the beep. I didn't leave a message but, instead, sent a text message.

Where R U?

No reply.

I stepped up to the box office at the movie theater.

"Which movie did they see?" I asked the girls.

"Some action-packed flick," Jade said. "I don't know the name of it."

I searched the movie board, looking for an action-packed movie that might have interested Vance. There weren't any, except for some Bruce Willis film, and the last showtime was at noon. Everybody who was anybody was seeing Tyler Perry's new movie, and according to the girl behind the counter, the previous showing had already ended.

"It was over twenty minutes ago," she said. "You wanna buy tickets for the next one?"

"No, thank you," I said and then joined my friends as they relaxed on a wooden bench outside of the theater.

"What you wanna do?" Indigo asked. "We were thinking about going over to Applebee's for some hot wings."

"That sounds good to me. Let's go." I tried to put a little enthusiasm in my voice. I didn't need to be stressing over Vance. Instead, I was going to enjoy my Saturday, with or without him.

At Applebee's we took the large corner booth, and each of us ordered iced teas with wedges of lemon in them. After our server placed our drinks on the table, we ordered three sampler platters filled with potato skins, quesadillas and hot wings.

The restaurant was full. Loud conversations and laughter filled the air. Our server was full of energy as she bounced from table to table, taking and filling orders. She wiped sweat from her forehead as she placed another glass of iced tea in front of me.

"Thanks," I said, and then she disappeared somewhere.

"Guess who tried to talk to me after the game on Friday night." Jade giggled.

"Who?" Tymia asked, crunching on the ice left over in her glass.

"Chocolate Boy?" Indigo asked teasingly, referring to Jade's ex-boyfriend, Terrence Hill.

"No! He's history." Jade frowned.

"Y'all didn't look like history at the party the other night," Indigo said.

"Whatever, Indi. I'm talking about Kendall Keller," Jade said.

"Kendall Keller, with the thick, pop-bottle glasses?" I had to ask.

"They're not that thick," Jade announced.

"What about the corny clothes and the ugly haircut?" Asia asked.

Jade was silent for a moment, and then stated, "He plays varsity," as if none of those other things mattered because of it. As long as he played varsity, it didn't matter if he looked like the bottom of my shoe.

"He plays varsity, but he rides the bench." Indigo dipped her quesadilla into a small dish of guacamole and stuffed it into her mouth.

"So what? I think he's nice." Jade smiled. "He has potential."

"He has a car," Tymia stated matter-of-factly. "That's a plus. And he's a senior."

"And he just walked in," Asia announced, and we all looked toward the door.

"Ooh!" Jade hid behind a menu.

"Why're you hiding?" Indigo asked. "I thought he was *nice*."

"Don't look now, but he's coming this way," I said.

As Kendall moved our way, he was followed by two other boys from the basketball team—both of whom were professional bench riders. They were on the basketball team, but never got any playing time. They weren't officially a part of the uncool crowd, but they weren't anything worth looking at a second time.

"Hey, Jade. How you doing?" Kendall asked as he stood next to our table. "You mind if we join you and your friends?"

Jade looked at our faces, her eyebrows raised and with a look on her face that said, Is it okay?

Before we could respond, the boys were pulling up chairs. Kendall squeezed in next to Jade. Lawrence Bell scooted way too close to me—I could actually smell his breath. Xavier Thomas wormed his way in between Indigo and Tymia.

"I couldn't remember if you said Applebee's or TGI Friday's," Kendall said and grinned at Jade.

It was obvious that the two of them had been talking. I'd never noticed, but Kendall had a nice smile, and his haircut wasn't really that bad. It actually looked freshly cut. And he wore jeans that sagged, with a colorful Sean John shirt. The glasses were pretty thick, though.

"Did y'all see Tyler Perry's movie yet?" Xavier asked.

"Saw it today," Tymia responded. "What about y'all?"

"I saw it on opening night," Lawrence said. "It was good."

"It is my favorite Tyler Perry movie yet," Xavier announced.

"Mine is *Why Did I Get Married?* That one has lots of drama," Asia said.

"No, the best one is *Daddy's Little Girls.* I wanted to kill those girls' mama and their drug-dealing stepdaddy!" Indigo said.

"Yep, that is my favorite, too," I said, agreeing with Indigo. I owned all of Tyler Perry's movies and plays and had seen *Daddy's Little Girls* at least five times.

"What is your favorite part?" Lawrence asked, his bright eyes looking right at me.

I'd never noticed Lawrence before—never even looked at him for any length of time. We'd had freshman literature together, but he never said anything in class. He would just make his way to the back of the classroom, place the hood of his jacket over his head and fall asleep every single day. I wondered if he'd even completed enough class work to make a passing grade. Here he was, asking me a question, when I'd never even heard his voice before.

"My favorite part is when Idris Elba takes Gabrielle Union to that club on Auburn Avenue...."

"And she gets so drunk," Lawrence added. "That was funny."

"Idris Elba is so fine!" Tymia exclaimed. "He could take me out any day of the week."

"What's so special about him?" Xavier asked.

"First of all," I began, "he's fine, tall, dark and handsome. And he has this sexy British accent…"

"All you looking for is a British accent?" Lawrence laughed and then changed his voice to sound British. "I got a British accent!"

We all laughed. Long and hard. As strange as it was for Kendall and his boys to join our table, we all had a good time. After they ordered another round of quesadillas and hot wings, we sat there for at least another hour, talking about school, movies and everything else that came to mind. We were so wrapped up in the conversation, I didn't even see Vance and Jaylen walk into the restaurant.

Vance looked good in his jeans and Grambling sweatshirt. His hair was perfectly trimmed, as usual. The way he licked his lips always reminded me of the way LL Cool J licked his. Vance's eyes met mine, and I gave him a half smile. He didn't smile back. Instead, he gave me a strange look. I waved, and he nodded his head.

"Isn't that Vance?" Asia asked.

"Yep, and Jaylen," Jade said.

Vance and Jaylen followed their hostess to a table on the other side of the restaurant. Vance didn't even come my way.

"I'll be right back," I said and stood. Made my way over to Vance's table.

"What's up?" he asked when I approached.

"What's up with you?" I asked, my hands on my hips. "Weren't you even gonna say something?"

"You looked busy," he said and picked up a menu.

"What do you mean?" I asked.

"You with Lawrence Bell now?" he replied.

"Excuse me?" I leaned back. "No, I'm here with my girls. They just made themselves at home at our table. Nobody invited them."

"Looks like they were invited," said Vance.

I decided to change the subject. Switch the conversation to him. "So what movie did you see today?"

"Tyler Perry's new movie. Why?" he said.

"Just you and Jaylen?" I asked.

"Hey, I'm going to the restroom," Jaylen announced and then got up from his chair. "Can you order me a Coke?"

"Yeah, man," Vance said.

"Just you and Jaylen?" I asked again.

"Just me and Jaylen what?" Vance asked as if he'd forgotten what we were talking about.

"The movies. You and Jaylen went to see Tyler Perry's new movie together."

"What's wrong with that?"

I shrugged. I couldn't find a thing wrong with that. And suddenly, I couldn't understand why I was standing at his table, questioning him, questioning us.

"I sent you text messages. And I've been calling you all day."

"My battery went dead, and I haven't been able to charge my phone."

"Somebody said they saw you and Jaylen at the movies with some other girls," I told him.

"Who said that?" he asked. "Jade, with her no-boyfriend-having self?"

"How did you know it was Jade?"

"Because I saw your posse over there at the movies earlier today, and Jade saw Jaylen talking to some girls from school," Vance said. "Jade should mind her own business."

I sighed with relief. Jade had misjudged what she thought she'd seen, after all.

"Did something change between us the other night?" I had to ask.

Friday night had weighed heavily on my mind since the

momentVance had dropped me off in front of my house. Everything seemed different now. Our relationship, our conversation. I needed to know that sex, or the lack of sex, hadn't driven a wedge between us.

"Can I get you guys something to drink?" the server asked as she approached the table, the name Jennifer plastered across her name tag.

"Two Cokes,"Vance answered.

"Make mine a Sprite," Jaylen said as he came back from the restroom, smiled at Jennifer. "Trying to watch my caffeine intake."

"I'll talk to you about it later," Vance said to me. "I'll call you when I get home."

"Okay," I said reluctantly.

I wanted to finish our conversation, but it wasn't the right place or the right time. Not to mention, as I glanced out the window, I saw my mom's car pull up. I'd forgotten that I'd sent her a text and asked her to pick me and my friends up at Applebee's.

There was no doubt thatVance and I would resume this conversation later. I wouldn't be able to sleep until we did.

ten

Tameka

I picked over my grits and eggs, on the verge of tears. Boy problems were never easy to deal with, especially when you really cared about the boy. My eyes were bloodshot from staying up almost the entire night, waiting for Vance to call or text. When I received neither one, my heart began to ache. I had blown it. He had moved on to someone else, someone else who was more willing to give it up.

"What's wrong, Tameka? Why aren't you eating?" my mother asked, pulling up a chair next to mine and putting her plate filled with bacon, eggs and grits on the table.

I played with my scrambled eggs. "Just not that hungry."

"Today is Lifetime movie Sunday." She smiled. "You ready?"

"Not today, Mom. I'm not really feeling Lifetime today."

"You look tired. Were you up late again?"

"A little."

"This is about a boy, isn't it?" she asked. She knew me too well. "Tell me what's going on. I can probably help."

"It's Vance." I was no good at hiding things from my mother.

She was my best friend. "I think he's messing around with another girl."

"And what makes you think that?"

"Well, Jade and Indigo said they saw him and Jaylen at the movies with some girls. Well, not Indigo. Jade said this."

"It sounds like a case of that he said, she said stuff. What did I tell you about that?" she asked, not really expecting an answer. She went to the refrigerator and reached for the orange juice. "Did you ask Vance if he was at the movies with another girl?"

"Yes. And he denied it," I said.

"Well, give him the benefit of the doubt," Mom said matter-of-factly.

"He was supposed to call me last night, and I didn't hear from him. No phone call, no text message. Nothing."

"That's why your eyes are red and you look like you're sleepy. This boy is under your skin." Mom plopped back down at the breakfast table. "Has he been in your pocketbook, Tameka?"

"No! Why would you ask me that?"

"Just checking. I told you about letting boys into your pocketbook before you or he is ready for it."

"He hasn't been." I stuffed eggs into my mouth.

"Okay, okay. I'm done asking," she said, "but don't forget what I said about it."

"I won't," I said. It was a conversation that was burned in my memory. How would I forget it?

The conversation stopped as my father stepped into the room.

"Good morning," he said. "How're my favorite two girls?"

"Good morning, sweetie," Mom said and locked lips with Daddy right in front of me.

I observed how they interacted with each other. Wanted to see if there was some tension between them. Everything seemed good on the surface, but I never knew what they talked about behind their bedroom door. Were they talking about splitting up? Did he know that Mommy was starting to resent him for being gone too much? Did he even care about her feelings?

"Morning, Daddy." My lips brushed against his rugged cheek. "Ooh, need a shave, don't we?"

"I'm letting it grow," Daddy said and ran his hand over his five o'clock shadow. He pulled the carton of milk out of the refrigerator. Poured a glass.

"How you like Mom's hair?" I asked.

"I, um, it's nice," he stuttered a little.

"It's very short, huh?" I asked.

"It's shorter than it usually is, but it's nice," my daddy said, carefully choosing his words.

That wasn't the response I'd been expecting.

Mom stuck her tongue out, and then pointed her French-manicured nail toward me. "Stop trying to start stuff, Tameka. And mind your own business."

"I was just asking if Daddy liked your hair." I smiled. "That's all."

The cordless phone vibrated on the countertop, and Daddy quickly grabbed it.

"Hello, uh. Yes, just a moment. It's for you, baby." He handed me the phone and headed out of the room. "And tell that boy not to call during breakfast anymore."

Boy? What boy would be calling me on the house phone?

"Hello," I answered.

"Good morning." Vance's voice rang through the phone and was like music to my ears. "So you're eating breakfast?"

"Yes."

"Want me to call you back?"

"No!" I exclaimed. "I was just finishing up."

I quickly took my plate to the sink, scraped the eggs and grits into the garbage disposal. I glanced over at my mom. At first, she gave me a cockeyed look, with raised eyebrows, but then she smiled.

"Is it Vance?" she whispered.

I nodded a yes and then headed out of the room, took the stairs two at a time to my bedroom.

"I thought you were gonna call me last night," I said. "What happened to that?"

"Well, I tried to call your phone all night, but I couldn't get through," he said. "That's why I finally called your house phone this morning."

"For real? You called my cell phone?" I searched for my phone, and once I found it, I flipped it open. The screen was completely black. I hit the power button. Nothing.

"I thought you were avoiding me," Vance teased.

Avoiding him? Not.

"No, my phone is dead. I need to charge it." I giggled and plugged my charger in. Relieved.

"I was thinking about going skating today. You wanna go?"

"Yeah. That sounds like fun." I accepted the invitation without even asking for permission from my parents, without giving any thought to what plans Mommy had for me.

"Can you meet me at Skate Towne later on, say, around three o'clock?" he asked.

"Yeah, I can do that," I said.

"See you then." He sealed the deal. "I'll holler at you later."

"Okay."

I pressed the power button on our cordless phone, held it to my chest.

No matter what had happened to us on Friday night, Skate Towne would make it all better.

eleven

Indigo

I bent over, panting; my hands touched my knees as I tried to catch my breath. I caught a glance at the muscles in my legs. It wasn't as if I hadn't worked for them; I'd done fifty sprints up and down the gymnasium floor each day before dance-team practice. With all our push-ups, sit-ups and crunches, we were in better shape than the boys' basketball team. Miss Martin insisted that there was more to dancing than just shaking our booties to music. Dancing was a sport, she'd explained, which meant that we had to stay in shape. It required exercise. She even encouraged us to maintain a healthy diet.

"Stop eating all those greasy foods, like fried chicken and pork chops. Grab yourselves a turkey sandwich, and ask your mamas to buy you some yogurt to bring for lunch," she'd smile and say. "And every now and then, you should consider a salad for dinner."

She must've forgotten who she was talking to. Fried chicken was a staple in most of our homes, and it was a crime if we didn't have chocolate cake or sweet-potato pie for dessert. Miss Martin knew that. She was just as black as the rest of us. I admired her for trying, though. But, honestly, I couldn't remember a time that my mother bought sliced turkey or those small cups of yogurt, which smelled like spoiled milk. The only time I was able to make a turkey sandwich was when we had turkey and dressing for Thanksgiving dinner, and Mama sliced the leftover turkey the next day and made sandwiches out of it.

I stood straight up as the cramp in my side started to ease up. I wiped sweat from my face and glanced over at Jade. She was breathing just as hard. Tameka pulled her hair into a ponytail and wrapped a scrunchie around it.

Miss Martin blew her whistle. "Okay, let's get started, girls. I do have a life, you know."

As Nelly's voice echoed across the gymnasium, I got a visual of his muscular arms holding on to a microphone and of him bouncing around onstage—tattoos plastered across his sexy body. I had rushed to the mall the day his new CD was released and had bought it. I'd stared at the cover for longer than I should have—stared so long, I'd felt like I was cheating on Marcus.

Everyone took their places as we began to practice our new routine. It was a number that our team captain, Kim Elliott, had created. That is, before she got pregnant and had to go to a different school. Mother High was the nickname they'd given to the school where pregnant girls went. I felt sorry for her. It must've been terrible getting pregnant just six months before graduation. I'd heard about people ruining their teen lives like that, but I didn't know anyone that it had actually happened to. It had been bittersweet, losing one of our best dancers, but with Kim gone, a spot had opened for a new team captain.

As the song faded, Miss Martin jotted notes down on a notepad. She looked up at us and began to pace the floor.

"As you all know, our team captain is gone," she said. "We're gonna miss Kim, but when we make adult choices for our lives, we have to live with the consequences of those choices. Kim's mistake should be a lesson to each of you."

I glanced over at Shelly Richards. There was a rumor that she had once been pregnant, but it had never proved to be true. Some folks said that she'd had an abortion, while others claimed that she'd never been pregnant. I never found out what the truth really was, but I was grateful that it wasn't me.

"I guess it's obvious that we will be looking for a team captain to replace Kim," Miss Martin continued.

I glanced over at Kelly Winslow as she ran her fingers through her silky flat-ironed hair, her lip gloss poppin' like Lil Mama's. Her muscular calves were twice the size of mine, and her breasts were at least three times my size. She was an okay dancer, but the truth of the matter was that she was a senior and had been on the dance team since ninth grade. Not to mention her mother taught algebra and geometry right there at Carver. Her mother, Mrs. Winslow, probably had lunch with Miss Martin every day in the teachers' lounge. She had an edge.

Then there was Missy Jones, also a senior. Her short and sassy spiked hair was as stiff as a board from all the spritz she used on it. She was tall and looked as if she could dunk a basketball. With her dark brown skin and flat chest, she could dance her butt off. It was no secret that she struggled to keep her grades on point. She'd almost gotten kicked off the team last year because of her grades. Miss Martin didn't play when it came to grades— if we failed our classes, there was no need to even show up for dance-team practice.

Miss Martin went on. "And instead of simply picking a senior for this spot, I think that we should give every girl on this team a chance to compete."

Kelly Winslow and Missy Jones looked at each other and then looked at Miss Martin as if she'd lost her mind.

"And so I'll be watching you over the next couple of weeks,

trying to determine which one of you is best equipped for the job," said Miss Martin.

Kelly spoke up first. "But, Miss Martin, the team captain has always been a senior."

"Yep, that's how it's always been, Miss Martin," Missy added.

"Well, not anymore, ladies," Miss Martin said. "Not necessarily. This time when I pick a team captain, it will be someone who deserves it based on talent, grades and character, and not simply because she's a senior. Now, let's run through the routine again."

As Nelly's voice bounced against the wall again, my heart began to pound. There was a chance that I could actually become the captain of this team, if I played my cards right. Jade and I looked at each other. I could tell that we were thinking the same thing. Just as I was thinking that I'd make the best team captain, Jade was probably thinking that she would, too. For the first time in our lives, we'd be competing against each other, and that felt funny.

After practice Jade and I stood inside to keep warm as we waited for her father's SUV to pull up.

"Did you see that stupid look on Kelly's face when Miss Martin said that the team captain wouldn't *necessarily* be a senior?" Jade whispered.

"Missy was shocked, too," I added. "Who do they think they are, anyway?"

"Seniors, of course," Jade said.

"Everybody knows I'll be the next dance-team captain." I snapped my fingers.

"Excuse me?" Jade's hand attached itself to her hip as she gave me a sideways look.

"You're excused," I said.

"Just think about it for a minute, Indi. Who did Miss Martin pick for the dance team, even though tryouts were over and done with?" Jade asked. "Me. And I didn't even have to compete with the rest of you stank females."

"If you recall, she only picked you because I begged her to."

"Whatever, Indi," said Jade. "We both know that's not true. She picked me because she knew I had skills."

"If you say so, Jade," I said and opened the gymnasium door, bracing myself for the cold air. "Your daddy's here."

"So, are you saying that I can't dance or something?" Jade asked as we walked briskly to her father's SUV.

"I'm not saying that," I said, suddenly wanting the conversation to end. It seemed to have taken a wrong turn somehow.

"Then what are you saying?" she asked, readjusting her gym bag on her shoulder and stopping in midstride.

"It is too cold to be standing out here, debating with you," I said. "Let's just drop it."

"Yeah, let's drop it," Jade said, and we both hopped into the backseat of her father's car.

"Hello, girls." Uncle Ernest turned and looked at our cold faces. "How was practice?"

"Fine." We both said it in unison.

"Hungry?" he asked.

"Not really, Daddy," Jade answered for both of us. "Can we just drop Indi off and go home? I have tons of homework."

"You don't want to stop for a burger?"

"No," Jade replied and stared out the window.

I hadn't meant to hurt Jade's feelings, but she had to know that I was a much better dancer than she was—any day of the week.

twelve

Vance

MY back against the locker, I tried with all my might to get a better grasp on my American history book and my three-ring binder. They were heavy, but I was determined not to ask for help. With crutches underneath my armpits, I was finally able to stuff the book and binder into my backpack. Wiping sweat from my temple, I limped quickly to my first class, plopped down in my seat and elevated my leg on the seat next to mine. With a cast covering the entire bottom half of my leg, I was left almost immobile.

"What happened to you, man?" Marcus asked as he entered the classroom and took his seat, right next to me.

"Skating."

Then he asked the dumbest question I'd ever heard in my life. "How you gon' play ball with a cast on your leg, dog?"

I glared at him. This was a very touchy subject to be discussing at such an early hour, especially since I'd already asked myself the same question a million times throughout the night. And considering I hadn't been able to sleep, I'd had plenty of time to come up with an answer.

"I can't play ball with a cast on my leg!" I snapped.

It was true. My basketball season was over. Twelve weeks on the bench would be like twelve years, and I wasn't happy about it. I had major attitude. Everything I'd worked hard for was about to be flushed down the toilet, and nobody really understood that except me. My parents obviously didn't know it, because they kept saying how temporary it was.

"You'll be out of that cast and back on the court in no time, sweetie," Mom had said right before she scribbled a red heart in the center of the cast.

"It'll be all right, son. Brush it off," Dad had said. "You already got a leg in at Duke."

"That's what you get for being so clumsy, stupid," my sister, Lori, had said, giggling as she scribbled her name on my cast with a purple marker. "You were probably trying to impress some stupid, ugly girl, anyway."

"Shut up, and get out of my room," I'd snarled. "And shut the door behind you!"

She'd placed her hands on her hips and rolled her eyes at me. After sticking her tongue out, she'd walked over toward the door. "I hope you're crippled for life," she'd said and then walked out the door, pulling the knob behind her.

"Don't slam…"

I hadn't been able to get the words out before my door slammed with a bang, and my framed Michael Jordan picture—the autographed one from his last Chicago Bulls game, when they played the Atlanta Hawks—had fallen from the wall and hit the floor. Glass had shattered everywhere, and I'd wanted to wrap my fingers around Lori's neck. What she'd said was right, though. I *was* trying to impress some girl. Tameka.

When I had arrived at the skating rink that day, Tameka was already in her pink-and-white skates, gliding backward on the floor. She waved when she saw me and came over to where I was, then plopped down on the bench beside me as I slipped my skates onto my feet.

"What's up?" I asked her.

"Nothing much. What took you so long?" she asked. "I've been here for almost an hour."

"I had to pick something up."

It was the truth. I had to run by the mall and pick up a necklace I had spotted on Saturday at the jewelry store. It was a sterling silver chain with a big, fat letter *T* dangling from it.

"Something like what?" She placed her hand on her hip and smiled her beautiful smile. I wanted to kiss her lips right there—and did.

After a quick little peck on her lips, I reached into my jacket pocket and pulled out the little white box. "Something like this." I grinned as I handed it to her.

She opened it, but not before giving me a cockeyed look. "Did you do something wrong that you need to be sorry about?"

"No, girl! I just wanted to give you something nice," I said.

The truth was, I *had* done something wrong. I had taken another girl to see a movie—not officially—but it was what it was. Although no PDA (public display of affection) had taken place, it hadn't stopped my hormones from losing control. Just the simple touch of Darla's fingers brushing against mine as we both reached for more popcorn had made the hair on my arm stand up. In the darkness of the auditorium, I had imagined her body against mine, her lips touching mine. And the fragrance that she'd worn hadn't helped matters at all. In an attempt to get those thoughts out of my head, I had rushed to the restroom at least three times.

I slipped the piece of silver around Tameka's neck, fastened the clasp.

"It's so pretty, Vance. Thank you," she cooed and then kissed my cheek.

"Let's skate," I said. "I need you to teach me how to do that backward thing."

"Okay, come on! It's so easy," she exclaimed.

Easy? Not. I fell on my behind so many times, it was ridiculous. And just when I thought I had it, I hit the floor—*again*—twisted my leg in an awkward way and landed flat on my back. As I was driven to the emergency room by my no-driving-skills-having girlfriend, Tameka, I feared for my life.

"I thought you told me you could drive!" I yelled as we soared down the street toward Grady Medical Center.

"I can drive!" she yelled back as she rolled quickly through a red light.

What had started out as a great day of skating had quickly turned into something else, and I wasn't feeling it at all. That was Sunday. How quickly things had changed. Now here I was, on crutches, and wishing I'd just taken Tameka to Steak 'n Shake for a burger and fries.

"Well now, Mr. Armstrong, what happened to you?" Mr. Harris asked.

"Skating," I mumbled. I was tired of people asking what had happened, and I was tired of answering. I just wanted to be left alone.

"Or not skating." He smiled. "Looks like you could use a little more practice."

As Mr. Harris headed back to the front of the class, I pulled my book out of my backpack and slammed it onto my desktop.

"Need some help?" Darla Union asked as she approached, wearing a short denim skirt with knee-high black leather boots, a cropped pink sweater and a black leather jacket. She looked sexy and smelled like the fragrance samples that came inside of magazines.

"Nah, I got it." I smiled.

"You mind if I sign your cast?" she asked, her pen in hand.

"That's cool," I said.

She drew a heart with an arrow through it, and inside the heart, she scribbled, Vance, Let Me Know How I Can Help U Heal. Much Love, Darla XOXO.

Snapping the top back on her gel pen with the purple ink, she winked and then took her seat, next to mine. I watched as she opened her book, not meaning to stare, but pink was definitely her color, and she was wearing it well. She was glowing, and I couldn't help but watch.

The thought of riding the school bus was already beginning to cramp my style, but it wasn't like I had a choice in the matter. It wasn't like I could drive, and with my parents' busy schedules, there was no hope of them transporting me back and forth. The school bus, which I hadn't been on since freshman year, was the only alternative to walking. The thought of it had me depressed the entire day. I'd thought about watching my team practice after school but decided I really didn't want to be depressed more than I already was. And since it was almost impossible to drive with my right leg in a cast, I figured my only ride home would be the big yellow school bus waiting next to the curb in front of the school.

"You gonna be okay?" Tameka asked as she walked me to the bus, struggling to hold on to my backpack.

"I'll be fine," I said. "I told you that you don't have to carry my books for me."

"I don't mind. You're my boo," she said and kissed my cheek.

If I am your boo, then why did you run away the other day, when we were about to go to the next level? I silently asked the question that had been burning in my mind for days. It had bothered me more than I'd let on, but instead of bringing it up, I'd let it fester.

I gave her a quick smile as we made our way across the courtyard to where the buses waited for students to board.

"Holler at me when you get home from dance-team practice," I said.

"I will." Tameka handed my backpack over.

I kissed her forehead and watched as she jogged back inside, her leotards hugging her thighs. Both crutches underneath one arm, I lifted myself onto the bus and plopped down in one of the seats up front, placed my crutches against the window.

As I glared out the window, I knew that this would be the longest twelve weeks of my life.

"Anybody sitting here?" Darla asked. Her leather jacket was zipped all the way up to her neck in order to shield her from the cold.

"Nah, just me." I slid closer to the window, and she plopped down in the seat next to me.

"Was that your girlfriend who just walked you to the bus?" she asked.

"Yep."

She leaned over me, pretending to look out the window. I guessed she was trying to get another glimpse of Tameka. While her breasts brushed against my arm, her fingertips traced the heart that she'd drawn on my cast earlier, and then her fingers moved toward my thigh.

"Does Tameka know how to take care of her man?"

The question came out of nowhere and threw me off guard. "What?"

"Does she do the things that girlfriends should do?" she asked.

I was dumbfounded and really didn't know how to answer that question. So I just said, "She's cool."

"I really like you, Vance. I wasn't sure if you could tell, but it's true." She smiled. "I wouldn't mind spending more time with you. Are you and Tameka serious?"

"Sort of, yeah." I was hesitant about the whole line of questioning.

What did I mean, *sort of?* Tameka had practically made me swear on a stack of bibles that I would be forever true to her.

That no other hoochie mama, as she called them, would come in between us.

"I guess what I'm really trying to say is, my mom works nights, and I'm usually at home all by myself every day after school." Darla grinned wickedly. "So anytime you want to come by, you can. We could hang out, watch some movies. We could do anything you want. And you don't even need an invitation."

"I'll keep that in mind." I pressed my backpack against my lap to hide the fact that Darla Union had me feeling things I'd never felt before and thinking thoughts that I shouldn't have been thinking.

thirteen

Indigo

I was giving it all I had, shaking everything my mama had given me as my hips swayed to the music. I wanted to show Miss Martin what I really had, just in case she'd forgotten. Every girl on the team was dancing better than she ever had, putting something extra into every move.

"Okay, girls." Miss Martin blew her whistle. "Give me one lap around the gym, and then we'll meet right here when you're finished."

I took off toward the bleachers. Marcus gave me his award-winning smile as I passed him. He was reclining on the bleachers, his gym bag in between his legs. His basketball practice was over early, and he was waiting for me, as he did most nights, watching our practice and giving unwanted advice about how I could make my routine better. I didn't show up at his practice, telling him how to shoot a free throw better or how to play better defense. Therefore, I didn't need dancing advice from him. Jade and Tymia jogged side by side and then caught up to me. Tameka and some other girls pulled up the rear. After we all completed one lap, we gathered around Miss Martin and waited for her to dismiss us.

"Great practice tonight, girls. You all are wonderful dancers, and I'm extremely proud that each of you is on this team. You each contribute to the team in a major way," she said. "And I really mean that."

"Have you decided on a team captain yet?" Tymia asked.

"As a matter of fact, I have...." Miss Martin smiled.

We all looked around at each other. My eyes bounced from Tameka to Tymia to Asia and then landed on Jade. She was crouched on the floor, tying her shoe.

"The young lady I've selected is someone who I think is best suited for the job. She has put in the work, her grades have improved tremendously and she has shown great character and a true spirit of teamwork."

She was right. I had put in some work. My grades were so much better than they'd been in my freshman year, and there was no doubt I had character. I was definitely a team player and had shown Miss Martin that just the other day, when I helped Keisha improve her routine. And even when she messed up, I was the one who encouraged her to keep trying until she finally got it.

"I believe that Jade Morgan would make the best team captain, and she is the young lady that I have selected," announced Miss Martin.

Did she say Jade Morgan? Surely I'd heard her wrong, I thought as I looked around at the other girls. I was waiting for someone to repeat what Miss Martin had said, just so I could confirm what I'd heard.

Jade stood up slowly. She was in disbelief, a shocked look on her face.

"It was a very difficult decision to make, because in my opinion, you all are team-captain material, but there was only one spot available," Miss Martin said, and then it was like she ran out of words. "So, I guess that's all I have to say. I'll see you all tomorrow. Same time, same place. We're performing the new routine at the game on Friday night, so practice your parts. Have a great night," she said. "Jade, I'd like for you to stick around for a few minutes, but the rest of you are dismissed."

My heart started pounding out of control. She really had said Jade Morgan was our new team captain. There had obviously been some mistake.

"Congratulations, Jade," Tymia said, and they gave each other high fives.

"Yeah, congrats, girl," said Tameka as the two of them embraced.

Everyone congratulated Jade except for me. I was still trying to gather my pride and force back the tears. Jade stared at me for a moment. She wanted me to congratulate her, but I couldn't. She had stolen my spot on the team. Miss Martin looked at me, too, as if she expected me to say something. She knew how tight we were, too.

"Congrats, Jade girl." Asia gave her a thumbs-up and then locked arms with me, pulled me toward the locker room. "Can I use your cell phone to call my mom?" she asked me.

I pulled my cell phone out, handed it to Asia as we left the gym. I didn't even look Marcus's way as I passed by, even though I could feel him watching me. He was always watching me, judging me.

With my feet on Marcus's dash, I messed with his radio. Tuned it to 107.9 as Young Jeezy's song rang through his speakers.

"You wanna talk about it?" Marcus asked.

"Nope," I answered and looked out the window.

"Indi, you should've at least congratulated Jade. That's your girl—your best friend," he said.

"It's unfair."

"It's Miss Martin's choice," Marcus said, "and you have to

be a true sportsman about it. Win or lose, you have to do the right thing."

"I said I didn't want to talk about it."

"Fine, but it's real childish to act that way," Marcus said, and his words pierced my heart. Whose side was he on, anyway?

"Are you calling me childish?" I asked.

"I'm calling the way you're acting childish, yes," he explained. "Your best friend made captain of the dance team and you didn't even congratulate her!"

"Are you going out with Jade Morgan or something? Whose side are you on, anyway?"

"I'm always on your side, but I have to let you know when you're wrong, Indi. I'm sorry," he said. "I love you."

Those three words melted my heart. Just as they had the first time he'd said them. I sat there for a moment, singing the words to the Young Jeezy song in my head. Then I pulled my cell phone out of my purse, flipped it open. Decided that Marcus was right. I should have at least congratulated Jade. It wasn't her fault that Miss Martin had chosen the wrong person for team captain. I sent Jade a text message.

CONGRATS. I typed it and felt a little better.

Waited a few minutes. I knew that she was in the backseat of her daddy's SUV—I'd seen her hop inside just minutes before Marcus and I had pulled out of the parking lot. She'd left the gym, yapping with Tymia, Asia and Tameka, probably telling them how she was so shocked that Miss Martin had picked her. I was shocked, too.

It's 2 late. Her text bounced into my in-box a few minutes later.

What do U mean, 2 late?

Keep UR congrats. It's 2 late.

"Who does she think she is?" I asked, not realizing that I'd said it aloud.

Marcus looked at me funny. "Who?"

"Jade." I frowned. "I told her congratulations, and she had the nerve to tell me it's too late. I only did it because you said I should. 'You're being childish, Indi. You need to congratulate her, Indi. She's your best friend, Indi.' Well, guess what, Marcus? I don't have a best friend anymore."

He just shook his head, watched the road and kept driving.

I pulled my coat tighter and crossed my arms across my chest, stared out the window and listened to the music. I was serious. I was through with Jade Morgan.

fourteen

Tameka

I was glad that practice had ended earlier than usual, and that I would be able to catch *106 & Park* from the beginning. After bumming a ride home with Indigo's father, Mr. Summer, I rushed into the house, took my shoes off and dropped my backpack at the front door. The smell of peach pie filled the house, and I knew that mom had finally popped that Mrs. Smith's pie into the oven. She wasn't much of a Betty Crocker herself, but she knew how to pick a good pie from the frozen-food section at Publix grocery store.

I went into the kitchen, opened the oven just to make sure that it really was peach pie that I smelled. The pie was almost golden brown, and my mouth began to water. I opened the refrigerator and grabbed a bottle of Coke. Heard music playing upstairs and followed it.

"Mommy!" I called.

I knew she was there, because her car was parked in the driveway.

"In here, sweetie," she said.

She sat on the edge of her bed, an open suitcase right next to her. Tears filled her eyes. My worst nightmare was beginning to unfold right before my eyes. Mommy was leaving Daddy for real. He'd really done it this time, spending too much time at the studio, never coming home. Mommy was fed up.

"What's wrong? Are we leaving Daddy?" I asked.

"What?" She looked confused. "No, baby. Why would you think that?"

"Well, you're sitting here crying your eyes out, and you're packing a suitcase. And you just said on Saturday that you were tired of Daddy's long hours."

"Tameka, your grandpa Drew had a heart attack."

Of all four of my grandparents, Grandpa Drew was my favorite. With his sense of humor, he kept everyone laughing nonstop. With a stomach that looked as if he'd swallowed a watermelon, he'd dressed up like Santa Claus and bounced me on his knee when I was little. My father had his eyes and smile, and I often imagined that when Grandpa Drew was much younger, he probably looked just like Daddy. He always told me funny stories about when Daddy was a little boy. I loved Grandpa Drew.

"Is he gonna be okay?" I asked.

"I don't know yet," Mommy said, "but Daddy's on his way home, and we're heading out soon. I need for you to go pack a bag."

"How long will we be gone? It's the middle of the week, and I have school tomorrow, not to mention dance-team practice and a game on Friday."

"Well, baby, you might have to miss school and dance-team practice for a few days." Mommy dabbed her eyes dry with a Kleenex. "This is an emergency."

"I know, Mom. And I'm sorry about Grandpa Drew, but couldn't you just go without me and let me fly up on Saturday or something?" I pleaded. "I have a game on Friday night, and I really don't want to miss it."

"I don't know about that, Tameka. You'll have to ask your father about that one."

"Ask her father about what?" Daddy walked into the room, dropped his car keys on the nightstand.

"She wants to stay here while we go to Charlotte," Mommy said.

"Hmm." Daddy looked at me. "You don't wanna go with us to check on Grandpa Drew?"

"I do, but I have a big game on Friday night. It's, like, the best game of the season," I said. "Maybe I could just fly up on Saturday morning or something."

"And how would you get to the airport on Saturday morning *or something?*" Daddy asked sarcastically, mocking me. "You want us to leave you the keys to the car, too?"

"Well, that's an option," I said. "I do have my driver's license, Dad. And I'm a good driver. I'm responsible."

"She is pretty responsible, Paul," Mom interjected, vouching for me. "I trust her to stay here alone, and she does pretty good with the car."

"It's a huge responsibility, baby," Daddy said. "You'd have to get yourself up in the mornings for school, get yourself to school and home from dance-team practice. You'll be here alone at night. You'd be responsible for making sure the house is secure when you're not here and when you are here. Then the whole airport thing. Parking the car, loading the luggage."

Was he trying to make me nervous, discourage me?

"I know all that, Dad." I hadn't really thought about it like that. I knew I'd be at home alone, but I didn't think about the reality of it—having to secure the house and such. That made me nervous. And the whole airport thing had me shaking in my boots. What if I missed the flight? There were so many small details to consider when traveling; I would be so scared that I'd miss something. But I still stood my ground. "I can handle it."

"Well, I guess I don't have a problem with it," Daddy said.

"Me, either," Mommy added. "And now that I think about it, there won't really be a need for her to fly up on Saturday if our plan is to return on Sunday night. Provided Grandpa Drew is out of the woods by then, we should be returning home pretty quickly."

"I agree," Dad said.

"We'll just play it by ear," Mommy stated. "See how things go. Maybe Grandpa Drew will recover, and we can come home sooner. But I think she'll be fine in the meantime."

"Under no circumstances are you to have anyone over here." Daddy laid down the rules. "You go to school, and you come home, Tameka. That's it. And you call us every day and let us know what's going on."

"I will. I promise you won't regret this," I replied.

"Let's hope not," Dad said, ending the conversation. "Please don't disappoint us."

"I won't, Daddy." I hugged his neck, kissed his cheek. I kissed Mommy.

She asked, "Can you get that pie out of the oven for me, Tameka? I need to finish packing."

I rushed down the stairs. Excited. I couldn't believe that they were actually going to trust me to stay at home alone. But then, I didn't know why I was surprised. After all, I was almost an adult—I was sixteen and a half, for crying out loud. Not to mention I was very mature for my age. Lots of people thought I was much older than I was. I could've easily passed for eighteen years old any day of the week. I pulled the peach pie out of the oven, set it on the stove. It smelled so good, and I quickly grabbed a plate from the shelf and cut myself a small piece. I let it cool, because it was piping hot. I sat at the kitchen table and smiled to myself. It felt good to be trusted, and I couldn't wait to have the house to myself.

As I finally ushered my parents out of the house, their luggage in tow, Mommy gave me last-minute instructions. Daddy literally had to pull her out the door. She was so worried about me that she called me before they even left the subdivision, and then again before they boarded their flight at Hartsfield-Jackson airport. After making sure that the house was secured, I sat curled on the sofa in the family room, a bowl of popcorn in between my legs, a tall glass of Coke on the coffee table. I flipped through the television channels. Decided to watch *Real Housewives of Atlanta,* just to see what those rich divas were up to. There was always some drama on that show.

When my phone buzzed, I knew it was Vance.

He sent a text message. Hey U.

I sent a text back. Hi.

WUP? Did UR homework yet? he asked.

Yes. Long ago.

Good.

Da parents went out of twn for da wknd.

Really?

Got da house 2 myself.

Cool. Then I can come ova?

Not 2nite.

Maybe 2morrow.

Maybe. After I texted him back, my father's voice was in my head. *Under no circumstances are you to have anyone over here.*

I sent Vance a yawn, just to end the conversation. :-O

G-Nite. CU L8TR.

G-Nite.

Just past midnight, and after I'd fallen asleep on the sofa, a noise shook me out of my sleep. I sat straight up for a moment, waiting to hear it again. Nothing. *Probably just the house settling, I thought.* I pulled myself up from the sofa, went upstairs to my room, slipped into my pajamas and collapsed onto my bed. I turned on the radio just to break the silence in the house, tuned it to the Quiet Storm on 103 and let it rock me back to sleep.

fifteen

Vance

I sat on the bench while my teammates made magic happen on the basketball court. Marcus had fourteen points by the second quarter, and I couldn't help wishing I was out there, lending him a hand. I felt like an idiot riding the bench. This was not how things were supposed to be going. When Coach called a time-out, the team rushed over and gathered in a huddle. As he gave my teammates instructions for the next play, my eyes wandered into the stands. Darla Union was seated in the stands, right behind our team. She smiled and gave a little wave. I gave her a little wave back. Just to be safe, I let my eyes wander across the gym toward the dance team. I wanted to see where Tameka was and if she was paying attention to me. I spotted her in the corner of the gym, running her mouth with Indigo, Jade and some other girls. She wasn't paying me any attention.

After the team rushed back out on court, I took my seat on the bench again and continued to watch the game. When my phone vibrated, I pulled it out of my pocket, looked at the screen.

WUD after da game? Darla asked what my postgame plans were.

Mickey D's. I responded.

It was where we all gathered after every game. My friends, including my girlfriend, would be there.

Can I come?

Suit URself. I'll be with my girl.

Wanna do something else? she asked.

Like what?

It's a secret.

It was no secret that Darla Union liked to play games. I was treading on thin ice with this girl, but she had me intrigued. I looked back at her in the stands. Gave her a smile and then turned to finish watching the game. Tried to clear away my thoughts of her, which were now cluttering my mind like cobwebs. She had my hormones raging.

After the game, Tameka and I found each other in the midst of the crowd. She hugged me around the waist, and I struggled to hold on to her and my crutches at the same time.

"We going to Mickey D's?" she asked.

"Yeah," I said, watching as Darla motioned that she wanted to talk. She headed toward the restrooms. "You go ahead to the car, and I'll just meet you in the parking lot."

"You sure?" Tameka asked.

"Yeah, I need to go to the restroom," I lied. "I'll be there in a few minutes."

I watched as Tameka buttoned her coat all the way up and exited through the gymnasium doors. I hopped toward the restrooms on crutches. Darla stood innocently with her back against the men's room door. She wore tight jeans and a shirt that hugged her breasts in just the right way. She grinned as I approached.

Everything inside me knew that I should've followed Tameka

to the car, headed to McDonald's and steered clear of all temptation.

"So what's up?" Darla asked.

"What's up with you?" I asked her.

"You goin' to Mickey D's or what?" she asked.

"What are my options?"

"Like I told you before, my mom works nights, so I have the place all to myself. We can go there and watch videos, or not," she said.

"You driving?" I asked.

"My car's right outside in the parking lot," she said. "You get rid of your girl, and we can be on our way to my place in a matter of minutes."

"Let me go handle my business," I said. The words just came out of my mouth before I could catch them. My mind was no longer in control, and my hormones were running this program. And hormones didn't seem to care if you had a girlfriend, or that her feelings would be hurt if she knew what you were up to. "I'll meet you in the parking lot in about fifteen minutes."

"Don't keep me waiting long." Darla's lip gloss was shining on her lips, and her sexy brown eyes made me want her more.

With that thought in mind, I headed for the school's parking lot. I had to do what I had to do.

sixteen

Tameka

Tears burned my cheeks as I stood with my back against the wall just outside the gym, listening as my boyfriend, the love of my life, the boy of my dreams, Vance Armstrong, made plans to be with another girl. It had just so happened that I needed to use the restroom, too, and I'd ended up coming back into the gym before I even got halfway to the car. As I'd approached the restrooms, I'd heard familiar voices and decided to eavesdrop. Something told me not to snap out right away, but to play it cool and to just listen for a few minutes. When you sat still and listened, you found out more than you ever wanted to learn sometimes. I was paralyzed as I waited for the best opportunity to make my presence known to both of them, and before I knew it, I was in tears. I wasn't supposed to be crying; I was supposed to be confronting. But I wasn't mad. I was hurt.

I slowly made my way around the corner, and my eyes locked with Darla Union's. I remembered our recent altercation and couldn't believe that she was the one who was pushing up on

Vance. I approached her, stood square in front of her and pointed my finger in her face.

"I don't appreciate you pushing up on my man!" I said.

"Then you should take better care of your man, little girl," she said. "If you did, I wouldn't have to."

She wouldn't have to? Did that mean she'd already taken care of him? Were they already messing around behind my back?

"I thought I put you in your place the other day," I told her.

"Apparently you didn't!" she snapped back.

I pushed her, and she fell against the restroom door. She lunged toward me in defense, and Vance stepped in between us just in the nick of time.

"Stop it!" he yelled and then grabbed my waist.

"Let me go!" I said and pushed him away. "We are so through, Vance." I walked away. Trying not cry, I was moving fast.

"Tameka, wait!" he yelled and reached for my hand, but I yanked it away.

I turned around just long enough to point my finger in his face. "Don't touch me," I said and then headed toward the glass doors in the gym.

Vance was moving quickly toward me, but since he was hopping on crutches, it was hard for him to catch up. "Tameka, wait up!"

I rushed out the door and never looked back. Left Vance behind in the cold Atlanta air. I practically ran to my mother's BMW, started the engine and burned rubber out of the parking lot. I needed to get as far away as I possibly could, and fast, because it felt as if my entire world had just fallen apart. Vance's words still stuck in my head. "Let me go handle my business," he'd told Darla. It was hard to believe that I was the business that he needed to handle. It was me that they probably laughed about when I wasn't around. I was the joke. That hurt.

I wanted to call my mother. She was my best friend and she would know exactly what to say. But I didn't want her worrying about me. I knew that if she thought I was in trouble, she'd be on the next flight from Charlotte to Atlanta in an instant, and I didn't want to inconvenience her like that.

Tears blurred my vision as I made my way through traffic on Old National Highway. When I finally saw our subdivision up ahead, I rejoiced. I was happy to finally pull into our garage and shut the door behind me. I was safe there. I could hide my pain from the world behind that garage door. I sat in the car for a moment, trying to get myself together, hoping that the pain would ease up just a little, but it didn't. I went inside, rushed upstairs to my room, threw my backpack on the floor, kicked my shoes off and curled up in my bed. I stayed like that for a long time. When the doorbell rang, it startled me. I got up, looked out my bedroom window, but didn't see a car out front. I couldn't see who was at the door, and it started to scare me. The person on the other side of the door was relentless and kept ringing the doorbell and knocking, and then my phone rang. I looked at the screen. Vance. Wasn't interested in talking to him, so I let it roll into voice mail. He called three more times before finally sending a text. I read the text.

I'm at da door. Pls let me in, he wrote.

I didn't respond. Just placed the cell phone on my dresser and sat on the edge of my bed, trying to figure out what to do next. He sent another text.

Please. Just want 2 talk.

Oh, now he wanted to talk. It seemed to me that he'd done all the talking necessary—to Darla Union, about God only knew what. Part of me did want to hear what he had to say, though. I wanted to hear that this was all a joke. Or that I hadn't heard things correctly, and they hadn't talked about hooking up. All of it had been one big mistake—maybe. I crept slowly down the stairs and made my way to the front door, leaned against it.

"What do you want, Vance?" I asked.

"I just want to talk, Tameka. Can I come in?"

With my back against the door, I contemplated letting him in.

"It's really cold out here," he finally said.

I slowly opened the door. He stepped inside, shivering from the cold. I closed the door behind him, folded my arms across my chest.

"What is there to talk about?"

"I'm sorry about tonight, Tameka. I didn't mean to hurt you, and I made a mistake."

"Yes, you did make a mistake. A big one," I said.

"It wasn't what it seemed. I promise."

"Then what was it? Because I heard everything loud and clear." I stood my ground. "Why were you trying to kick it with someone else?"

"I don't even know," he said, not even denying the fact that he was trying to kick it with someone else. "I don't even like her like that."

"You just wanted to sleep with her, huh?"

He shrugged. I was right. He wanted to sleep with her, and it hurt knowing that.

"I'm sorry, Tameka. I never meant to hurt you," he said. "And I don't want to lose you."

He reached for my hand, and I didn't pull away this time, but I didn't look at him, either. I looked away. He grabbed both of my hands in his, held on to them. Then he pulled me close, and I relaxed in his arms. My mind was telling me to pull away, throw him out and tell him where to go, but I didn't. Instead, I let his lips touch mine.

"What does she have that I don't, Vance?" I had to ask. Insecurity had found its way to my heart.

"She doesn't have anything on you. Nothing at all," he said.

"Then why were you all up in her face, making plans with her?"

"Just stupid, I guess." He sounded so sincere, I couldn't help but believe him. "What we have is really special, and I almost messed it up."

"Yes, you did!"

"Will you forgive me?"

I ignored his question and asked, "How long have you been messing around with her?"

"I'm not messing around with her," he said. "I'm with you, Tameka, and you only. She wants to get with me."

"Have you slept with her?" I asked.

"No. I promise I haven't," he said.

"But you were willing to," I said.

"I'm not gonna lie, Tameka. I was thinking about it. And I'm sorry…"

My heart started aching, and I didn't know how to make it stop. The thought of him thinking of another girl in that way made me sick.

"If I make love to anyone, I want it to be with you," he said.

I believed him. He wrapped his arms tightly around my waist and kissed me with passion. I put my arms around his neck. He didn't know it, but I had already forgiven him. And when his fingers began to caress my skin, I didn't even stop them from roaming.

"Where's your room?" he whispered.

We had reached that crossroads again. It was the same cross-roads that we'd found ourselves at before, only this time there was a little twist. I could send Vance away, but there was a chance that he would end up in Darla Union's arms in a matter of seconds. She was probably somewhere waiting for that to happen, hoping I would turn him away. She wanted to get her claws into Vance and steal him away. And I wasn't about to let that happen.

"My room is upstairs," I told him. "You have to take your shoes off in the house."

He removed the Jordans from his feet. His hand in mine, I led the way upstairs to my bedroom.

"Nice room," he said as he looked around.

"Thanks." I smiled. Who would've dreamed that Vance Armstrong would be standing in the middle of the floor in my bedroom, saying that my room was nice?

I hit the power button on my stereo, popped in Lloyd's CD, and ironically, his "Love Making 101" track rang out across the room. Vance didn't waste any time pulling me close again, and our lips locked—*again*. Before I knew it, I was lost in the moment. There was no turning back. We slow danced in the middle of my floor, and then Vance led the way to my canopy bed. We both sat on it slowly, careful not to let our lips come apart.

"I brought protection," he whispered.

I was glad, because protection was important if we were going to move to the next level. It seemed that this was actually going to happen. His lips against mine, his fingertips all over my body, our hearts beating at a consistent pace, we became one in an instant—one love, one mind, one soul. As the song encouraged us with its lyrics, we made love to the music. And when we were done, Vance held me in his arms, and we both fell asleep.

The sound of Vance's ringtone shook the room. He and I sat straight up. We looked at each other; both of us were dazed for a moment. He grabbed his cell phone from my nightstand.

"Oh, snap, it's three o'clock!" he exclaimed.

"In the morning?" I asked, wiping sleep from my eyes.

"I gotta get home. That was my father calling," he said, searching for his jeans. He pulled them on, buttoned them. "I caught a ride over here with Jaylen. You think you can you take me home?"

"Right now?"

"Yeah, right now."

I'd already broken the rules—had company over when my

dad had specifically asked me not to. Now Vance wanted me to drive my parents' vehicle in the middle of the night, when I was told not to go anywhere but school and back home. I had taken so many chances already.

"Yeah, I'll take you." It was already out there before I could take it back.

The streets of College Park were dark and quiet, reminiscent of a ghost town, as I took Vance home. My heart pounded the whole way. There wasn't much to talk about at that hour, and so there was silence in the car. He grabbed my hand and intertwined his fingers with mine. I felt safe, felt lucky. Like I had won the prize and Darla had lost. I wished she could see that Vance belonged to me, in every way. His heart belonged to me.

I finally pulled up in front of his mini mansion. The neighborhood was so quiet that you could actually hear the crickets chirping in the night. I lowered my headlights so they wouldn't disturb any of his neighbors.

"I'll call you when I wake up," he said. "You wanna check out a movie or something? We can go to the matinee."

"That'll be cool."

"All right." He opened the door and stepped out of the car. "Send me a text and let me know that you made it home."

"I will."

I watched as he approached his front door, used his key to go inside. When I saw the upstairs light pop on, I pulled away quickly. Made my way back home, driving just below the speed limit, as my mind drifted back to the intimate moment I'd just shared with Vance. We had been so natural with each other. It had felt right. Vance didn't need to go anywhere else. He had everything he needed right here.

seventeen

Indigo

It had been five days, seven hours and twenty-eight minutes since I'd last spoken to Jade. We were officially on non-speaking terms, and it felt weird. There hadn't been many times that we'd been apart. Just the time that she had the chicken pox and I had to stay away; and the time that I had that stomach virus, and her mother wouldn't let her come over and play Barbies with me. Then there was that time that she moved to New Jersey to live with her grandmother. That was probably the longest time we'd ever spent apart. And even then, we talked on the phone just about every day.

But now, when I saw her in the hallways at school, she walked past without so much as a hello. And I wasn't about to say anything. In my opinion, she was the one who was being childish, rolling her eyes like I had done something wrong. She needed to grow up.

As I stood in the lunch line, holding my plastic tray, she walked past, running her mouth with Tymia and pretending that she didn't even see me standing there.

"Can we have a cut, Indi?" Tymia asked.

"You can." I responded directly to Tymia, making sure that my body language expressed who I was talking to—and not talking to.

"I didn't ask her for a cut, anyway. So I don't need her doing me any favors," Jade said, with her back to me. "Tymia, let's just go to the back of the line. We don't need her."

"Tymia, you are definitely welcome to cut in front of me if you want to," I said.

"We're just gonna go…you know…back there, to the end of the line, Indi," Tymia said. I could tell she felt uncomfortable being in the middle of our catfight. "You're welcome to join us at our usual table by the window. Okay?"

Jade was already heading to the back of the line, and Tymia followed.

"Okay." I said it sadly. Now she was stealing my other friends away, too.

"Hey, girl!" Tameka entered the cafeteria, wearing jeans and Vance's basketball jersey. Something was different about her. She wore her hair pulled up on her head, instead of her usual flat-ironed style. She approached me in line. "Can I get a cut?"

"Yeah, you can," I said and then spotted Asia, who was running to catch up with Tameka.

"There's Jade and Tymia in the back of the line," Asia said. "Let's go back there."

"Come on, Indi," Tameka said, and grabbed my arm. "Let's go back there with them."

Reluctantly, I followed them to the back of the line, where Jade and Tymia stood, with their trays. The usual giggles and gossip began the minute we all got together, but it was obvious that Jade and I were not speaking to each other. Whenever we had something to say to or about each other, we said it in third person.

"I saw Kim the other day at Publix," Asia said. "She's starting to show."

"You mean, she actually looks like she's preggers?"

"Yes, big-time," Asia said.

"I bet she's pregnant by that boy who dropped out of school. The one who used to hang around our dance-team practice, waiting for her," Jade said.

"I wonder if her baby is going to be dumb, since he obviously was," Tymia said.

We all laughed.

"Everybody that drops out of school is not dumb, Tymia," Tameka clarified.

"They are in my book," Tymia insisted. "Anybody who makes it all the way to the twelfth grade and then drops out *is* dumb!"

"My mom dropped out in the tenth grade because she was pregnant with me," Tameka said, "and my mom is not dumb!"

"She was pregnant with you in the tenth grade?" Asia asked.

"That's our age," Jade said.

"I would die if I got pregnant in the tenth grade!" Tymia exclaimed. "I can't even imagine it."

"Your whole life would change." I added my two cents. "You wouldn't be able to do anything. No parties, no dance team."

"You would even have to go to a new school," Asia announced. "Can you imagine wobbling down the hall in front of all your classmates—fat and preggers?"

"I'm too young to be anybody's mama," Jade said.

"Can you imagine me asking Marcus, 'Where's my child support?'" I laughed, because it sounded so ridiculous. "And this baby need some Pampers…and some formula! Don't stand there looking at me crazy, boy. Go on down to Wal-Mart and get some."

Everybody laughed. Even Jade. I thought about Kim. Wondered

if she was wobbling down the halls of her new school. Wondered if she knew who her baby's daddy was, and if he was going to help her take care of the baby once it was here. I wondered how she was going to take care of the baby once it was born. Would she get a job, or would her parents help her out? I wondered how mad they'd been when they found out. What if they had kicked her out of the house, and now she was wandering aimlessly through the streets of College Park, looking for a place to sleep? I felt bad for her and thanked God that it wasn't me.

Jade and I managed to get through the entire lunch period without even mumbling a word to each other. We avoided even looking at each other. I was grateful for my other friends, because otherwise it would've been a pretty lonely world. I liked her hair that day, though. She'd obviously tried something new with it. And the outfit she had chosen for the day was hot. I still remembered where she bought it—Charlotte Russe at Cumberland Mall. That was where she got the jeans. And she bought the tangerine-colored top at Forever 21, off the clearance rack, end of season. I had a blue one just like it. But I wasn't about to tell her that her outfit was cute. The compliment that was dangling around in my head would never reach my lips. In fact, I looked the other way before she caught me checking out her gear.

In Mr. Espin's Spanish class, I dozed off at least three times before he finished going over our homework assignment—which I didn't have, by the way. The fourth time that I dozed off, Mr. Espin stared right at me, but the fifth time, he tapped me on my shoulder.

"Didn't get enough sleep last night, Señorita Summer?" he asked.

I tried to focus my bloodshot eyes on Mr. Espin.

"I'm awake," I said.

"Do you have your homework?" he asked.

I began searching through my three-ring binder, pretending to look for it. I already knew it wasn't there, knew I hadn't done it. I had been too busy gossiping on a three-way call with Tameka and Tymia the night before. We were on the phone until at least one o'clock in the morning, and by the time I hung up, I was way too tired for Spanish homework. I struggled in Spanish more than I did in math. I didn't get it, and Mr. Espin seemed to forget that we weren't born in Cuba, like he was. It took a while to grab hold of a new language, especially when we didn't even have English down yet. I was still working on my English prepositions, pronouns and verbs.

"Um, I think I left it at home," I lied.

"Or maybe the dog ate it?" he asked sarcastically.

"I don't have a dog, Mr. Espin." I wasn't in the mood for his sarcasm. I hadn't completed my homework. So what? What was he going to do? Give me a detention?

"Señorita Summer, you may serve a detention in the cafeteria after school," he said.

"Are you serious? You're giving me a detention for not having my homework?" I was wide-awake now.

"And for falling asleep in my class," he said.

"I can't serve a detention, Mr. Espin. I have dance-team practice right after school. And I can't miss practice." I pleaded my case. "And besides, a detention will get me two demerits. And I can't afford that. I might not get to perform at the game on Friday night."

"Señorita, you should think about these things before blowing off your homework," he said. "My class is just as important as your dance team. You should put forth just as much effort."

"This class is just so hard, Mr. Espin. I don't get Spanish."

"Then you should ask for help," he said. "In the meantime, I will see you after school. And in the future, please try and be more prepared for my class, Indigo."

Was he trying to ruin my life? Miss Martin didn't play when it came to grades and discipline. She would kick you off the team so fast, your head would spin. She was very strict in that area. I had to find a way around this.

Dance-team practice had already started, and here I was, straggling in thirty minutes late. I'd already had Tameka and Tymia cover for me. They were supposed to tell Miss Martin that I was sick, and that I would be in the nurse's office, resting for a little while. If I felt better, I'd be late for dance-team practice.

"She's not gonna buy it, Indi," Tameka had warned. "And I don't really like lying to Miss Martin like that. You're gonna get me some demerits, too."

"What if she sends someone to the nurse's office to check?" Tymia had asked.

"She won't," I'd insisted. "Miss Martin is too busy to be worrying about my whereabouts. Please, y'all. Help a sister out."

"Why don't you just make up with Jade? She's the team captain. She's the only one who can cover you, Indi," Tymia had replied.

"I'm not making up with her! She needs to make up with me," I'd said. "I'll take the demerits first."

"Fine, Indi. I'll do it." Tameka gave in. "But if I get in trouble for covering—"

"You won't get in trouble. I promise," I'd said.

"I'm not playing," Tameka had said.

"This is not cool," Tymia had said. "Why didn't you just do your Spanish homework?"

"Because I was on the phone with y'all hoochies last night," I'd reminded them. "Talking about your little, ugly boyfriend with the nappy hair."

We had spent most of our chat time trying to tell Tymia what a loser her new boyfriend was. He was already starting to accuse her of other boys, and they weren't even exclusive yet. And he was already starting to be aggressive with her, pulling on her arm. He even shoved her once. In my opinion, that was a red flag. He would've been history the first time he grabbed my arm. But she liked his smile. A million boys at this school had a nice smile, and she had to pick the weird one.

"Whatever, Indi," Tameka had said. "I'll do it, but it better not backfire on me."

"Thank you!" I'd been so grateful. I was home free.

I stepped into the gymnasium and then walked slowly toward center court, where the group was practicing a new routine.

"Miss Summer, we're glad you could join us," Miss Martin said. "You can begin with your laps around the gym, and then take a seat in the bleachers."

Laps? Was she serious? Didn't she get the word that I was sick?

I took off around the gym, slowly. I panted as I finished the first lap. I tried to read the faces of my friends Tameka and Tymia. Wanted to know if the lie had gone over or not. Tameka was into her routine. She didn't even look my way. She took dance way too seriously, in my opinion. With a serious look on her face, she shook her hips from side to side. Tymia finally looked my way, and I tried reading her face. When she shook her head from side to side, I knew something was wrong. But what?

After running my last lap, I bent over and tried to catch my breath. Then I took my seat in the bleachers, as Miss Martin had suggested. When practice was over, she dismissed the team and then motioned for me to come see her.

"Why were you late, Indigo?" she asked.

"I, uh, I wasn't feeling well in my last class, so I went to the nurse's office for a little while."

"Which nurse's office was that? Because when I sent some-one to check on you, she couldn't find you." Miss Martin's mouth was moving, but I blanked out for a minute.

"Um…" I didn't even have a response.

"She did, however, find you in the cafeteria, serving a de-tention," Miss Martin said. "And you know how I feel about detentions. They are for students with behavior problems, and none of my girls have behavior problems."

"Miss Martin, I'm sorry for lying. It's just that Mr. Espin gave me a detention for nothing. I didn't have my homework, but I told him that I don't understand Spanish and I need help. It's not fair to give somebody a detention for not having their homework when they don't understand it."

"Indigo, you know what my rules are. I don't really care about the circumstances surrounding a detention. A detention is a detention, as far as I'm concerned. And the consequences are just that…consequences. You can't perform at Friday night's game."

"Aw, Miss Martin, not Friday night's game! We been prac-ticing that hot routine. I wanna dance," I pleaded. "Please let me dance."

"Indigo, you know the team rules. If I let you get away with it, then what kind of example would I be setting for the other girls on the team? That's what I was looking for in a team captain, someone who would be an example for other girls. Not someone who tried to use their friends to lie for them. You understand?"

I nodded yes.

Her decision seemed final. She seemed unmoved, and it was worthless to keep trying to convince her to give me another chance. I gave in.

"Am I dismissed?" I asked.

"You can go now," she said.

I lifted my gym bag onto my shoulders and headed for the locker room. I wondered who had given me away. Was it Tameka or Tymia? I stopped in my tracks, turned to face Miss Martin.

"Who told you that I had a detention?" I asked.

"My new team captain, of course. Jade," she said.

Jade was the one who had snitched on me?

"I sent her to check on you because I know how close the two of you are. It took great character for her to come back and tell me the truth. Most friends would lie for each other. But Jade didn't, and I was proud of her. You could learn a lot from her, Indigo. Jade is a wonderful role model."

Didn't she mean Benedict Arnold?

eighteen

Tameka

GRANDPA Drew's heart wasn't as strong as I thought it was, because somewhere between my late-night conversation with Vance and the wee hours of the morning, it stopped pumping. When Mommy crept into my room and gently touched my hair, I knew something was wrong. She sat on the side of my bed; the tears on her face glistened in the moonlight.

"Wake up, baby," she whispered.

"Grandpa Drew?" I asked. I already knew.

"He had a second heart attack, but he couldn't survive this one. He passed away," she said. "But he didn't suffer long."

Tears began to fill my eyes. I thought about Grandpa Drew and how funny he was, and realized that I would never see him again. I would never hear him tell his corny jokes again, or hear his laughter. He'd always laughed at his own jokes. He would wrap his arms around me and tell me not to worry so much.

"You worry too much, ladybug," he would always say. "Don't be so serious all the time. You're just a kid."

"I'm not just a kid, Grandpa. I'll be sixteen on my next

birthday," I'd told him when I was fifteen, grinning from ear to ear.

I was fifteen when I'd last seen him. I suddenly wished I had gone with my parents to see him when he had his first heart attack. At least then I could've talked with him again. I could've heard one more of his silly jokes. I could've said goodbye. But now all I had were memories.

"How's Daddy?" I asked Mommy. "Is he okay?"

"I had to call him at the studio. He's on his way home." Mommy wiped tears from my eyes with her fingertips, but they kept flowing.

"I can't believe that he's gone. It just doesn't seem real," I cried. "I just called him two weeks ago to tell him about my grades. He was so proud of me."

"He loved you so much," Mommy said, "and even though he's gone, he still lives right here in your heart." She touched the center of my chest.

"It's so weird, because when you and Daddy came home a few weeks ago, he was doing so much better," I whispered in between tears.

It was true. After my parents had come back home from checking on Grandpa Drew, he had been doing better. The doctors had been so positive, telling us that he would recover as long as he changed his diet, but they obviously didn't know Grandpa Drew like I knew Grandpa Drew. He loved to cook, and he loved to eat. And he loved to eat stuff that wasn't good for him—like lots of butter and fried foods. He could eat a loaf of bread in a couple of days' time. And he didn't know a thing about exercise. He would walk outside to get the newspaper or the mail, but that was about it.

Tears began to flow like a river. My face was soaked from just thinking about Grandpa Drew.

"We're going to North Carolina for a few days," Mommy

said. "We'll probably leave in a little while. You'll have to go with us this time, Tameka. You might have to miss a few days of school. And that means dance-team practice, and probably a game, too."

"I wanna go, Mommy. I need to say goodbye to Grandpa Drew," I said.

"Why don't you start getting packed. And make sure that you take one of your Sunday dresses."

"For the…funeral?"

It was weird saying the word *funeral* while talking about Grandpa Drew. It gave me a funny feeling. It was the same feeling I'd gotten when Mommy said, "He passed away." It was almost as if she was referring to someone else. It was like when you watch the news, and they talk about people dying in car accidents or people who are murdered. You didn't really give it a second thought, because it was no one that you knew. It was not someone who had bounced you on his knee when you were a little girl. It was not somebody who had kissed your forehead and squeezed you tight before tucking you into bed. It was not the person who you had made milk mustaches with or the person who had tickled your feet until you'd almost wet your pants.

"Yes, for the funeral," Mommy said. It was hard to believe that Grandpa Drew was really gone.

After Mommy left, I stared at the ceiling for a while. I felt a little numb and wanted to just lie still for a moment. Wanted to try and picture my grandfather's smile, but couldn't. I wondered if he would become just a distant memory in my mind. I hopped out of bed, opened my closet and pulled a shoe box down— the one that held stacks and stacks of pictures that I'd collected over the years. I sat on the edge of the bed and sorted through the photos until I found one of Grandpa Drew. It was a photo of him reclining in his easy chair, a big smile on his golden-brown face. I smiled at the photo, and then tears filled my eyes.

I wanted to change the mood, so I popped a CD in and bounced to the music. I pulled my overnight bag out of the closet and started filling it with underwear and socks. Then I packed a few pairs of jeans and a couple of sweat suits with the cropped jackets. I gathered my CDs and stuffed them into my CD case. I placed various bottles of Victoria's Secret shower gel and lotion into my overnight bag. I packed everything except for a dress. Couldn't bring myself to pack that.

After I pulled myself out of the shower, I slipped on a pair of sweats and a polo shirt with the Aéropostale butterfly on the breast. I pulled my hair into a ponytail and rubbed some lip gloss on my lips. I slipped on my sneakers and sat on the edge of the bed.

"Ready?" Mommy appeared in my doorway, looking adorable in her pink sweat suit, with a brown shirt underneath. Her funky haircut was looking hot.

"Yes," I answered.

"You okay?" she asked and sat on the bed next to me, wrapped her arm around my shoulder. "We're all gonna miss him."

I nodded a yes.

"Which dress did you pack?" Mommy asked.

There was the issue of the dress again, the dress that led to the funeral. The funeral that led to the reality that Grandpa Drew was really gone. I shrugged my shoulders.

"Baby, you have to pack a dress," she said, "unless you're gonna wear your Apple Bottoms to the services."

I cracked a smile but really didn't feel much like smiling. "I don't know what to pack."

"Are you kidding?" Mommy headed for my closet. "All those dresses you have. You need to pick one. And let's get moving. Your daddy's warming up the car. We're about ready to pull out."

She left the room and shut the door. I searched my closet

for a dress. I would wear a dress, but it wasn't going to be black or any other dull color. This would not be a sad occasion. Grandpa Drew enjoyed life, and I wouldn't make this dull for him. I would wear red or pink. Maybe I would even wear a white dress. I grabbed dresses in all three colors, stuffed them into my bag.

"Are you ready, baby?" Daddy met me at the top of the stairs, grabbed my bag.

"Yep," I said.

"How you holding up?"

"Good." I kissed Daddy's cheek. "How you holding up?"

"I'm doing fine, baby. Thanks for asking." Daddy placed his arm around my neck, and we headed down the stairs arm in arm.

I could tell this was going to be a long weekend, for both of us.

nineteen

Tameka

IN the backseat of my parents' SUV, I listened to one of Rihanna's CDs while flipping through the latest copy of *Vibe* magazine. I wasn't really reading. My mind was a roller coaster of thoughts. I wondered if Grandpa Drew was in Heaven yet. Wondered if he'd gone there immediately, or if he'd waited around for a little while. Maybe he was waiting for us to get there, to say goodbye.

I wondered if Vance would miss me. Wondered if he would hook up with Darla while I was gone, or if he would stay true. He'd promised to keep in touch while we were apart, but I couldn't help wondering if I could really trust him. After all, I'd given him an intimate part of myself, just so he wouldn't have to go looking for it somewhere else. I pulled up his photo that was stored on my camera phone, stared at his cute little smile. I hoped and prayed that our relationship could withstand these few days apart.

I pulled up the calendar on my cell phone. It was the seventh day of March, and my visitor hadn't paid me a visit yet. My visitor was my menstrual cycle, which usually paid me a visit on the first day of every month. It was like clockwork—I never missed it, and I was never late. But here I was, seven days past due, and I was nervous about it. There was no way I could be pregnant. After all, Vance and I had used protection. We had taken every precaution to do things the right way, so I dismissed that thought altogether.

My phone vibrated. I'd received a text from Vance.

WUP? he asked.

On my way to NC. Grandpa Drew passed away.

He knew who Grandpa Drew was. I talked about him all the time.

Sorry 2 hear dat.

Thx.

U OK?

Yes.

I will miss u.

Ditto. The truth was, I missed him already.

As we pulled up in front of Grandpa Drew's house, my heart started pounding uncontrollably. I knew that my grandfather wouldn't be rushing to the car to greet us, as he usually did. He wouldn't even be inside waiting for us, with a piping-hot meal on the stove—some concoction he'd gotten off the Food Network. He wouldn't be reclining in his easy chair. Inside, I would find only Aunt Helen, my daddy's oldest sister, and my cousins Jason and Roni, who had lived with Grandpa Drew. Aunt Beverly was probably on a nonstop flight from Cincinnati, and Uncle Rich and his family would be driving up from Florida.

"I'll get the luggage later," Daddy said as he stepped out of the car.

Aunt Helen stood on Grandpa Drew's front porch, an apron tied around her waist.

"Is that my little Tameka?" she asked, obviously forgetting

that I wasn't *little* Tameka anymore. I was a sixteen-year-old, high-school-going, driver's-license-having Tameka. I was one year older than her daughter, Roni, so she should have known that I wasn't a little girl anymore.

"Hi, Aunt Helen," I said.

"Give me a hug," she said. "You're growing up to be so pretty."

I hugged her tightly, and when she finally let go, she hugged my parents.

"Something sure smells good, Helen," Mommy said.

"Well, I knew that you all were coming, so I threw a casserole in the oven. Come on inside and take a load off." Aunt Helen went inside and headed straight for the kitchen. "Jason! Roni! Come on down here and say hello."

Roni rushed downstairs. A much shorter version of me, she wore her hair similar to mine, flat ironed and hanging on her shoulders. She wore a tight pair of jeans and a Guess T-shirt.

"What's up, Tameka?" She smiled, a pink cell phone glued to her ear.

"Hey," I replied.

"Where's your brother?" Aunt Helen demanded.

"I don't know. Upstairs, being stupid, I guess," Roni said. "Hi, Uncle Paul and Aunt Mel."

"Hi there, Roni," Mommy said.

"The jeans are a little bit tight, don't you think?" Daddy asked Roni and then turned to Aunt Helen. "You let her wear stuff like that?"

Obviously, he hadn't seen some of my jeans and how they hugged my hips. He was usually asleep when I left for school in the mornings and still at work when I came home from school. He might not approve of lots of my outfits were he to see them.

"That's how they're wearing the jeans now, Paul. Tight and slender at the ankles," Aunt Helen said. "Not much different from Mel's little outfit over there."

Aunt Helen smiled at Mommy, but Mommy didn't smile back. It was no secret that Aunt Helen was a little bit jealous of Mommy's figure, especially since she didn't quite have one. Aunt Helen reminded me of the comedian Mo'Nique, with her oversize hips and her large breasts. She was always well dressed, and her hair was always together, but she shopped in the big women's section of the store. And deep down inside, I believed that she was jealous of my mom's curves.

"Hey, girl, if you got a figure like mine, why not wear something to enhance it?" Mommy asked and then sashayed toward the kitchen. She seemed to be taunting Aunt Helen with her size-seven Apple Bottoms jeans and Apple Bottoms top, which hugged her just right. She never let Aunt Helen get to her. "Now, let me go on into this kitchen and see what you got cooked up in here, Helen."

It was no secret that Daddy's oldest sister, Aunt Helen, didn't care much for Mommy. Aunt Helen resented my mother for getting pregnant with me at the age of sixteen and ruining my daddy's future—or at least the future she thought he should have. He was supposed to go to college and maybe even become a lawyer, but instead, he'd ended up dropping out of college, getting married and becoming a father at a very young age. Aunt Helen had thought my mother was too fast for Daddy. After all, Mommy had grown up on the opposite side of the tracks. With a single mother who sang in nightclubs, Mommy hadn't been good enough for my daddy in Aunt Helen's opinion. She'd tried keeping them apart, but it hadn't worked. They'd been too much in love, and there was nothing she could do about it.

Grandpa Drew had raised his children alone, since his wife died after giving birth to Aunt Beverly. My daddy and his siblings never even knew their mother, and I often wondered if Aunt Helen might've turned out better if she'd had a mother figure. Maybe then she wouldn't have so much resentment from having to help raise her younger brothers and sister. Because she'd been forced to be a mother figure at such an early age, she went around trying to be everybody's mama.

"Let's go upstairs. *106 & Park* is on," Roni said and then headed up the steps.

I followed her upstairs to one of the guest bedrooms in Grandpa Drew's house. It was so weird walking up those stairs and past my grandfather's bedroom, knowing that he wasn't there anymore. I stopped in front of his bedroom door, looked inside. A pair of his khaki pants was lying across the bed, and his ties were still hanging on the closet door.

"I hate that he's gone," Roni said. "I miss him already."

"Me, too," I said. "I wish I had come when he was sick. Then I could've at least said goodbye."

"I wonder whose gonna protect me now," Roni said.

"Protect you from who?" I asked.

"From the barracuda lady down there," she said, referring to her mother, "and from Lucifer."

"Who's Lucifer?" I asked.

"Never mind," she said and changed the subject. "Did you get those jeans at 5.7.9?"

"The Gap," I said. "Clearance rack."

In one of the other guest bedrooms, my cousin Jason sat on the edge of the bed, crouched in front of the television, playing a video game. He never looked up as Roni and I stood in the doorway.

"Hey, J," I said.

"What's up, Tameka?" he asked, his eyes never leaving the television.

"Didn't you hear barracuda lady calling you?" Roni asked him.

"What does she want?" he asked, his eyes still steady on the TV.

"Go find out!" Roni said before moving on to the third

bedroom, where I could hear *106 & Park*'s host, Terrence J, introducing the next musical guest who was appearing on the program's Freestyle Friday competition.

The bedroom, which was painted soft pink, was the one I had shared with my cousins Roni and Alyssa since we were toddlers. Aunt Helen had decorated the room especially for us. When we were five, she had the Powerpuff Girls all over the wall. When were ten, it was SpongeBob who danced on the walls. And once we became teenagers, the cartoon characters that were painted on the walls were replaced by posters of Omarion, Usher and Mario—our three favorite entertainers.

"Terrence J is so fine." I grinned and then plopped down on one of the twin beds, remote control in hand. I propped the pillow behind my head.

"He's a'ight," Roni said and then bounced onto the bottom bunk across the room. We always left the top bunk for our younger cousin, Alyssa. We always slept in the exact same beds when we visited Grandpa Drew's house.

Alyssa, who was on her way from Florida with her parents and younger twin brothers, would probably have pictures of Usher all over her cell phone. She would carry one of his CDs around in her purse, asking if we could listen to it a million times. While Roni and I could pass for sisters, Alyssa looked more like her mother's side of the family—lighter skin, long, curly hair and light brown eyes. She was much skinnier, too. Aunt Helen was always trying to fatten her up with smothered pork chops and mashed potatoes and gravy. Alyssa played just about every sport that her school offered—basketball, volleyball and soccer. She was an all-around athlete and was sure to get a scholarship somewhere. She wanted to attend Spelman with me, but of course, her parents wanted her to stay closer to home and attend one of the universities in Florida.

Roni, on the other hand, didn't participate in any extra-curricular activities. Not anymore. She had once been on the cheerleading squad and the volleyball team at her school in Charlotte, but when her grades took a nosedive she was kicked off both teams. After Aunt Helen decided to get married during Roni's freshman year in high school, Roni's behavior did an about-face. She started getting into trouble at school, and her grades were so horrible, she almost got held back a grade. She did whatever it took to make her mother miserable, and I couldn't count the number of times Aunt Helen called my daddy for him to "talk some sense into Roni," as she put it. She'd even sent Roni to Atlanta to spend a couple of weeks at our house during the summer, just to see if that would help her behavior. My mother had said she was the perfect angel; she just needed some attention and a little bit of TLC. The moment Roni went back home, her behavior went right back to being horrible.

It was no secret that Roni hated her new stepfather, Grant, like she hated green peas—green peas made her throw up. He was always barking orders at Roni and Jason, like they were animals instead of human beings. When they complained to their mother, she would simply say, "You need to get used to Grant being around. He's not going anywhere." And that seemed to depress Roni all the more. She was convinced that Aunt Helen was blind to who the real Grant really was.

"He's a bastard," she told me once. "And he cheats on my mother. I know who it is, too."

"How do you know?" I'd asked.

"I just know," she'd claimed.

"Have you told Aunt Helen?" I'd asked.

"She wouldn't believe me," she'd said. And that was how we'd left it.

★ ★ ★

As I watched *106 & Park,* it was hard to stay awake. I needed toothpicks to hold my eyelids open, and since I didn't have any, I let them fall shut. Gave in to the sleep fairy and dozed off completely.

twenty

Indigo

The mall on a Friday afternoon was more like a morgue. Nobody hung out there during the week. I was anxious to return the jeans that I'd picked up at Macy's during their one-day sale, and since I didn't want to go to the mall by myself, I dragged Tymia along for the ride. Daddy agreed to drop us off and pick us up in an hour, while he ran over to Home Depot for tools to fix our upstairs toilet. Once inside the department store, we headed straight for the juniors department, in search of a pair of jeans that actually looked better on than they did on the hanger.

"And this time you should try them on before we leave the store," Tymia said. "Don't just assume they're gonna look right."

"I plan to," I said and started sorting through the jeans rack.

Tymia and I danced to John Legend and Andre 3000's song "Green Light," which was playing over the speaker system. She actually knew the words and sang along—loudly.

"We should do a routine to that song," I teased.

"We should," Tymia said. "It's a nice song."

"It sounds like pop or rock, and not at all like John Legend," I said. "Is he getting weird or what?"

"He's a little different," Tymia agreed, "and Andre 3000 has been weird."

"The routine would go something like this," I said and started moving my hips as I made up something as I went along.

"That's good, but we need to add a little bit of this." Tymia started moving to the music and mocking my routine, but she added a few steps of her own.

An older saleswoman walked over just in the nick of time, her glasses at the tip of her nose. She was much too old to be working in the juniors department. She couldn't have known anything about young adult fashion.

"May I help you ladies?" she asked.

"No, we're fine," I answered, "but thank you."

Now go away. That was what I wanted to say, but I bit my tongue instead.

"Let me know if you need some help," replied the saleswoman.

She slowly walked away, and Tymia and I continued to bounce to the music. It was hard finding a pair of jeans that was within my budget, but I finally located a pair that was just a little more than I was willing to pay.

"Here. Hold my purse while I try these on," I told Tymia.

The jeans were perfect. I turned to get a better glance at my butt in the mirror, slipped my hands into the back pockets. They were definitely going home with me, I thought.

When I stepped out of the dressing room, Tymia was busy talking to Asia and who else? Benedict Arnold, of course—aka Jade Morgan. I walked up behind Tymia, grabbed my purse from her shoulder.

"Hey, Asia," I said, completely ignoring Jade.

"What's up, Indi?" Asia asked. "You're returning those jeans you bought the other day, huh?"

"Made my butt look flat," I said.

"That didn't take much," Jade mumbled under her breath.

"What you say?" I asked Jade, with attitude. I wasn't sure if I'd heard her right, but it had sounded like she'd said, "That didn't take much."

"I wasn't talking to you." Jade had attitude right back.

"Yeah, but it sounded like you were talking about me," I said.

"So what if I was?" Jade hissed.

"Then say it to my face." I was in her face within seconds.

"I'm not afraid of you, Indigo," Jade said and stood her ground.

"No, you're just afraid of Miss Martin!" I yelled. "So much so that you have to snitch on your friends."

"My friends?" she asked. "Are you calling yourself my friend?"

"Not anymore," I said. "With friends like you, who needs enemies?"

Asia stood in between us. "Those jeans are cute, Indi. Do they look cute on?" She was trying desperately to change the subject, defuse the fire that was already burning inside me. I didn't have time to discuss jeans with Asia. I was fired up and needed to get some things off my chest.

"You could've covered for me that day when I had a detention. That's what friends would do!" I continued with the argument.

"You shouldn't have gotten yourself in detention. You know how Miss Martin feels about problems," Jade said, sounding more like a school administrator than someone who had once been my best friend. "You put me in a bad position."

"This dance-team-captain stuff has gone to your head," I said and tapped my finger right on her forehead.

"Don't put your hands on me," she warned. "I think you're just jealous that you're not the team captain."

"Jealous of who? You?" I asked. "Everybody knows I'm a way

better dancer than you. Not to mention my grades are better," I snapped. "I'm a better team player—"

"But your attitude stinks!"

"Your attitude stinks, you two-faced, brownnosing…"

Before I knew it, we were on the floor in Macy's, rolling around like guests on *The Jerry Springer Show.* Asia was pulling Jade off me, and Tymia was holding on to my arms to keep me from swinging again. The department store's security guard was on his walkie-talkie as he approached; his counterpart followed close behind. The two of them dragged us both off, through the store.

"Call my daddy!" I yelled as I tossed my cell phone to Tymia. "His number's in my phone."

The saleswoman who'd tried to help Tymia and me earlier looked on as Jade and I were taken away like common criminals. A frown on her face, she shook her head in disgust. "I knew they were trouble the minute they walked in here," she said as we passed.

I rolled my eyes at her. Wished she would get hit by a truck.

twenty-one

Tameka

when I felt something crawling on my face, I gently brushed it away. I felt it again and brushed it away again. The third time, I gave myself a slap on the face and then sat straight up in bed. Giggles filled the room as my twin cousins, Nick and Nate, stood over me. It was the tail of Nate's toy dinosaur that had been crawling on my face.

"Are you gonna sleep forever?" Nick asked.

"Not with you two in the house," I said.

They both giggled.

"Can you hook up the PlayStation in here for us, Tameka?" Nate asked.

"No!" Roni walked into the room and answered for me. "If you wanna play video games, you need to go in the room with Jason."

"He won't let us play," Nick whined.

"Too bad." Roni stood firm. "You can't play in here. We're about to watch *Real Housewives of Atlanta* reruns."

"Hey, Tameka," Alyssa greeted me as she walked into the

room, carrying a paper towel filled with potato chips. She hugged me, and I grabbed a chip.

"When did y'all get here?" I asked.

"About an hour ago," Alyssa said. "Aunt Helen wanted us to wake you up for dinner, but your mom said to let you sleep."

"The barracuda lady can really get on your nerves sometimes." Roni rolled her eyes and then started surfing through the television stations.

"All the adults are goin' over to the funeral home to plan Grandpa Drew's funeral," Alyssa said.

There was that word again—*funeral*. I didn't like it, and I didn't want to think about it.

"So what's been going on, Alyssa?" I asked. "You still messing with that boy that Uncle Rich chased down the street when he caught him in the house?"

Roni and I laughed.

"Nope. I got a new boyfriend," Alyssa announced. "He's fine, too. Plays football."

"Your high school football team sucks," Roni said.

"He doesn't play for my high school team." Alyssa smiled. "He plays for FAMU."

"He's in college?" I asked.

I wanted to protest, but the truth was, I had been in her shoes before. I had dated a boy who was a freshman at Morehouse College when I was a freshman in high school. He was supposed to be a senior in high school, but he'd skipped a grade. So technically, he was a senior in high school and not really that much older at all.

"Shh, not so loud," Alyssa said. "I don't want those two little rug rats in there all up in my business. All I need is for my daddy to find out."

"I know what you mean," I said. "My daddy is the same way. He thinks that I'm still a little girl sometimes."

"I know. I hate it!" Alyssa exclaimed. "I'll be fifteen in a couple of months."

"I don't know, Alyssa. How old is this dude? Eighteen? Nineteen?" Roni asked.

"He's nineteen." Alyssa grinned.

Roni and I were both in shock. Our mouths opened at the same time; our eyes were the size of saucers.

"Oh my God! Nineteen?" I asked.

"You dated a boy who went to Morehouse, Tameka!" Alyssa reminded me.

"He wasn't nineteen," I clarified. "He was seventeen. He was supposed to be a senior in high school, but he skipped a grade. So that doesn't count."

"Well, excuse me," Alyssa said. "T. J. is just so mature. He's not like the stupid little boys who go to my school."

"Of course not. He's a grown man!" Roni said. "Dude can vote if he wants to."

"And he did vote...for Barack Obama, thank you very much!" Alyssa snapped her fingers as if she'd just said something brilliant.

"Are y'all having, you know, sex?" I had to ask. "Because if so, he could go to jail, you know."

"We haven't yet, but I'm thinking about it," Alyssa said. "What about y'all? Are y'all having it with your boyfriends?"

"I don't have a boyfriend," Roni stated, and both of them looked my way for my response.

Alyssa smiled. "Well, Tameka? Inquiring minds want to know."

I couldn't help blushing.

"You don't have to answer," Roni said. "We already know by the look on your face."

"Okay, I won't," I said.

"Please tell me that you are using protection," Alyssa said.

"Of course," I mumbled.

"Aha!" Alyssa said. "So you are having it."

"We did it one time," I finally admitted.

"We?" Roni asked.

"Me and my boyfriend, Vance," I said. "He's a senior in high school, Alyssa. He's not in college."

"When…?" Roni asked. "When did it happen?"

"A couple of weeks ago. When my parents came down here to check on Grandpa Drew when he had his first heart attack," I said. "Vance came over. We popped in a Lloyd CD—"

"Lloyd!" Alyssa and Roni said it at the same time, and then both of them giggled.

"What's wrong with Lloyd?" I asked. "They were love songs!"

I could always share things with my cousins that I couldn't share with anyone else in the world. Not with my mother… not with my girlfriends. My cousins and I had started sharing things when we were five. They were like the sisters I'd never had. Whatever we shared never left the walls of our pink bedroom. There were secrets that these walls had kept for many years—like the first time Brandon and I had rubbed up against each other, or the first time Roni had kissed Tyler, French-kissed. And the walls still held the details of the time that Alyssa had showed Kevin her pink-and-white panties in Grandpa Drew's backyard—and Kevin had showed her his tighty-whities. The older we got, the more serious the secrets became.

"Why didn't y'all listen to some Usher?" Alyssa asked. "With his fine self."

"Or some Robin Thicke!" Roni said.

Alyssa jumped onto the bed and got closer to me. "How was it?" she whispered.

What an embarrassing question, I thought as I could feel my face turning beet-red. If ever there was a chocolate-brown girl that could turn beet-red, it was me.

"Quit. You're embarrassing her," Roni said.

"I want details! I'm still a virgin, and I wanna know if it's even worth it to go there," Alyssa said.

"You're still a virgin? With a boyfriend in college?" I asked.

"Yep, for now," Alyssa admitted. "Roni, you're a virgin, too, right?"

Roni looked away as if hiding something.

"Roni," I said, "you are still a virgin, right?"

"Let's change the subject." Roni's face became serious.

"Are you holding out on us?" Alyssa asked. "Tameka, she's holding out on us."

"I'm not holding out! I just don't want to talk about it." Roni left the room, and I could've sworn she was crying. The bathroom door slammed. Something wasn't right.

Alyssa and I looked at each other, dumbfounded.

"What was that?" I asked.

"I don't know," Alyssa said.

And that was the end of that conversation.

A family meeting was called when our parents returned, and the details of Grandpa Drew's funeral arrangements were shared. The service was scheduled for Saturday afternoon at the church where we attended Sunday school when we were little kids. Two family cars would pick us all up at the house and drive us to the church.

The conversation turned sort of eerie when Aunt Helen said, "The funeral home did such a nice job of embalming him, don't you all think?"

A nice job of embalming him? Was she crazy?

"Mom, that's kinda gross." Roni rolled her eyes and said what I was thinking.

"Well, they did," Aunt Helen insisted and then turned to her brothers, my daddy and Uncle Rich. "I think we should bury him in his navy-blue suit. The one he wore to Rich and

Annette's wedding. And I like his red tie, the one that I bought him for Christmas last year."

"Well, I like his gray pin-striped suit. It's not so dark and gloomy," Aunt Beverly interjected. "And I can't stand that red tie."

"Well, the gray suit doesn't really go with his skin color that well. He always looked so handsome in navy blue," Aunt Helen said.

"Daddy didn't wear dark colors. He was a happy man, and I think we should bury him that way," Aunt Beverly said.

"It doesn't really matter to me what he wears," Uncle Rich stated. "It's not gonna matter after the coffin is closed, anyway."

"Well, we need to decide for the services," Aunt Helen snapped. "People are gonna see him there, and he needs to look nice."

"Let's ask Mel and Annette," my daddy said.

Mommy smiled at Daddy. "I tend to agree with Beverly. Daddy Drew was a happy and upbeat man, and a gray suit sounds much better."

Aunt Annette, with her Puerto Rican accent, spoke up. "The gray suit does sound a little better to me, too."

Aunt Helen stood. She looked upset. "I think the decision making about my daddy should be left up to his children, not his daughters-in-law," she said.

Mommy and Aunt Annette looked disappointed. Grandpa Drew had loved them both like daughters, and he would've been upset at Aunt Helen for excluding them from anything. Luckily, they knew how Aunt Helen could be sometimes. Besides thinking that my mom had ruined my daddy's future by getting pregnant at sixteen, she also thought that Uncle Rich should've married someone from his own race. Although Aunt Annette was mixed with two races, African-American and Latina, it was the Latina side that Aunt Helen had a problem with.

"Daddy loved Mel and Annette as if they were his own

daughters, Helen. You know that," Aunt Beverly said. "But if you insist on a decision coming from his blood children, then I vote for the gray pin-striped suit."

"Me, too," Daddy said.

"Gray sounds better to me also," Uncle Rich stated. "And personally, I like his burgundy silk tie. The one he wore to your wedding, Helen."

"Fine. I guess I've been outvoted, then. Y'all can bury him in whatever you want to. I don't really care," Aunt Helen said and then headed for the kitchen. "Children, you need to go get washed up for dinner."

At the dinner table everyone ate in silence. So much sadness in a house where there had once been so much joy.

twenty-two

Indigo

IN the security office at Macy's, I waited for Daddy to come and rescue me. I was angry as I peered across the room at Jade. Her chest moved up and down as she breathed heavily. She was waiting for Uncle Ernest to come and rescue her. It was hard to believe that Jade and I had come to this point when we'd once been like sisters. Our families had lived next door to each other for years. I'd eaten at her house a thousand times, and she at mine twice as many times. I couldn't remember how many sleepovers we'd had, or how many times we'd come to this very mall—together. We'd created a million dance routines and gone trick-or-treating more times than I could remember. We'd borrowed each other's clothes, CDs and jewelry and never returned any of them.

Daddy had that usual frown on his face, a wrinkle in between his eyes. I knew that frown all too well. It was the one that he usually got when I'd really messed things up. It was a look of disappointment.

"Indi, what's going on?" He looked at me and then at Jade, a puzzled expression on his face. "Jade?"

"Hi, Uncle Harold," Jade said softly.

"Hello, sir." The fat security guard stood, reached for my father's hand. "I'm Officer Jones."

"Harold Summer." Daddy shook his hand.

"Which one is yours?" Officer Jones asked.

"That one." Daddy pointed my way. "What has she done?"

"She was involved in a physical altercation with this young lady," said Officer Jones. He pointed at Jade.

"You mean a fight?" Daddy was shocked and confused all at the same time. He looked to me for an answer, but I really didn't know what to say. I just shrugged to let him know that what the officer had said was true.

"They didn't cause any damage to the store, and the store management has decided not to press charges, considering they are minors," Officer Jones said. "However, I did have to call the local police, and they are on their way over. They're gonna want to question the girls, and I'm not sure if they'll want to charge the girls with disturbing the peace or—"

"Let me get this straight," Daddy said. "You mean to tell me that these two young ladies—this one and this one—were fighting each other?"

"That is correct, sir," Officer Jones stated. "Right in the middle of the store."

"Whoa." Daddy exhaled, lifted his baseball cap and scratched his head. "What's this about, Indi?"

I just shrugged.

"Jade?" Daddy said. He looked her way for an answer. "What do you two have to say for yourselves?"

"Sorry?" It was more of a question than a response that Jade offered.

Uncle Ernest walked in, still wearing his work clothes—gray slacks, a starched white shirt and a colorful tie. Jade's little sister, Mattie, held on tightly to his hand. She wore white tights underneath her green, white and blue plaid school uniform.

"Jade, what's up?" Uncle Ernest asked immediately, and then his eyes scanned the room. "Harold, what's going on?"

"Well, apparently the girls got into a fight at Macy's," Daddy began. "Neither one of 'em seems to have anything to say. So I don't really know what to make of it."

"Hello, sir. I'm Officer Jones." The security guard reached for Uncle Ernest's hand. "I'm holding the girls here until the local police arrive. They were involved in an altercation...."

"With each other?" Uncle Ernest was just as shocked as my dad had been.

"Yes, with each other," Officer Jones said. "They didn't do any damage in the store, and store management has decided not to press any charges, but the local police will need to take a report. They'll probably just release the girls to your custody."

I was embarrassed. What had seemed like a good reason to knock fire from Jade an hour ago seemed silly now. Especially with both of our fathers looking at us as if we'd just got done murdering somebody.

"I'm disappointed," Uncle Ernest said, "in both of you."

"That makes two of us," Daddy chimed in.

Jade sat in a chair across the room. Her shirt was ripped, and she held it together with her hand. Her hair was all over her head, and there were scratch marks all over her arm. I held a wet paper towel against my busted lip. I felt my ears for my hoop earrings; the left one was gone.

When the Morrow police officer showed up, pen and pad in hand, I just knew we'd be arrested. He questioned me about the incident, and then he questioned Jade. Then he introduced himself to our fathers. He told them that we were free to go, but that we would have to appear in juvenile court. All of this because Miss Martin had picked the wrong person as dance-team captain. If she'd just picked me, all of this could've been avoided.

The ride home was quiet and uncomfortable. Daddy didn't bother to say anything to me, except to ask if I was cold. When I nodded a yes, he pumped up the heat and warmed the car.

After we arrived home, I tried to tiptoe up the stairs to my room, but my father's voice stopped me in my tracks.

"Wait a minute, young lady," he said. "We need to talk."

I knew it was coming—a lecture. Especially when he'd been completely quiet the whole ride home, except for when he'd run down all the details for my mother on his cell phone. Outside of that, he hadn't mumbled one single word. He'd probably spent that time thinking of how he was going to punish me.

Mama wiped her hands on a kitchen towel and followed me into the family room. I sat on the edge of the sofa, Daddy sat in his recliner near the window and Mama just stood.

"I need to know what on earth would make you and your best friend since grade school get into a fistfight," Daddy started. "In the middle of Macy's department store, for chrissake!"

When he yelled, I jumped.

"I, um, it all started with Miss Martin," I said.

"Miss Martin?" Mama asked. "The dance-team coach? What does she have to do with this?"

"Um…she chose Jade as team captain a few weeks ago. And it wasn't a fair choice. I'm a much better dancer than Jade, and she knows it."

"And?" Daddy was being impatient.

"And Jade's been acting all funny lately. And she came up in Macy's, talking junk, like she's all cocky and stuff! She's changed since Miss Martin made her the team captain. She's not even the same Jade anymore." I embellished, but just a little. "She said my butt looked flat, and that's when I lost it."

"She said your butt looked flat?" Mama asked. "That's what this is about?"

"Yes, ma'am," I replied.

"Indi, that is ridiculous!" Daddy yelled.

"I don't really know what to make of all this, Indigo Summer. But Barbara and Ernest are having this same conversation with Jade right now. I imagine that Jade's details are probably just a little different from yours," Mama said, "but we'll get to the bottom of this somehow."

"In the meantime, though, of course, you know you're grounded, right?" Daddy asked.

"Yes, sir." I'd already kind of figured that out.

"That means no cell phone, no sleepovers, no extracurricular activities," Warden Daddy said. "You will go to school and come straight home. You will do your chores, complete your homework and then go to bed…in that order."

"For how long?" I asked cautiously, ready to duck in case somebody wanted to swing.

"Until further notice," Daddy said.

"Do you have homework right now?" Mama asked.

"I have math homework, which I need Marcus to help me with," I said.

"Well, that won't happen." Daddy stood. "You won't be seeing Marcus except at school."

"Can I still ride to and from school with him?" I asked.

"You will ride the bus to school in the morning. And your mother or I will pick you up from practice at night." Daddy added, "That understood?"

"Yes, sir," I mumbled.

"You can go on and get started on that homework, then," Mama chimed in.

"I need help with it," I pleaded, hoping they would understand the importance of my talking to Marcus—at least one more time.

"I'll come up and help you myself," Daddy volunteered. "I'm not a math whiz like Marcus, but I can solve a problem or two."

Daddy helping me with math? This was going to be the worst punishment ever. Life as I knew it was over.

twenty-three

Tameka

With my pjs on, I sat on the side of the bathtub in the small bathroom. After checking to see if my visitor had decided to show up and discovering that it was still late, I flipped open my phone and checked the calendar again. It was now eight days past due, and the clock was steadily ticking. I shut my phone and then splashed cool water on my face. The loud banging on the door startled me.

"I gotta use it!" Nate yelled.

There was never a moment's peace at Grandpa Drew's house, especially when Nick and Nate were there. I swung the door open, and Nate was on the other side, dancing around in his SpongeBob SquarePants pajamas. He shot right past me and commenced to pull down his bottoms.

"Well, good morning to you, too," I said, leaving the bathroom and shutting the door behind me.

The smell of pork sausage and bacon filled the house. Blueberry muffins were definitely in the oven, and knowing Aunt Helen, there were homemade biscuits, cheesy eggs and fresh fruit on the table, too.

"Meka, can you help me take my pajama shirt off?" The other twin, Nick, had met me in the hallway in his briefs, with his pajama shirt halfway over his head.

I pulled it off for him. "There you go, squirt," I said.

"Thank you!" he yelled and then took off down the hallway in his underwear.

In the pink room, Roni was still curled up in the bottom bunk, light snores creeping from her mouth. In the top bunk, Alyssa sent a text message to someone, probably her much-older boyfriend, T. J.

"Good morning," I said to her.

"Morning," Alyssa said, never looking up from her phone. "Aunt Helen wants us to come down for breakfast. I tried to wake Roni up, but she's not budging."

"Roni!" I shook her.

Roni rose up in bed and looked around in a daze. "What? What?"

"It's time for breakfast," I said.

"Oh," she growled and then plopped her head back down, smashed a pillow into her face. "Tell the barracuda lady I'm not hungry."

"Come on. Get up!" I insisted. "Let's eat and then get dressed. I want to go over to the mall today. Maybe my dad or Uncle Rich can drop us off."

"Too late for that," Alyssa said. "Uncle Paul and Daddy went to play golf this morning. They're not back yet."

"Well, whose car did they take?" I asked.

Alyssa peered out the window. "Your dad's car is in the driveway."

"Cool. Then my mom can take us to the mall," I said.

Roni pulled herself up from her bed. "What is with you people? It is too early in the morning for idle conversation." Roni was definitely not a morning person. There were days that she could actually sleep until noon if someone let her. I liked sleeping in on the weekends, but after a while your head started feeling funny. Too much sleep was never good.

I started straightening my bed and fluffing my pillow. I threw my overnight bag onto the bed, unzipped it and searched for something to wear. I decided on my Ecko Red jeans and a matching top. I selected my hoop earrings and a new bra and panty set that I'd picked up at Victoria's Secret.

Mommy appeared in the doorway. "Don't worry about getting dressed, girls. Aunt Helen wants you downstairs at the breakfast table right now. Just wash your faces and brush your teeth. You can come down in your pjs."

"Wouldn't wanna keep Mother waiting," Roni said sarcastically. She slipped a pair of house shoes on her feet and headed out of the room.

Alyssa hopped down from the top bunk.

"Mommy, can you take us to the mall after breakfast?" I asked.

"That should be fine," Mommy said and slipped one arm around my neck and the other arm around Alyssa's neck. "We don't really have any plans for the day, and I'm sure you girls are bored to death."

Aunt Helen stood facing the kitchen sink. Her new husband, Grant, held on to her waist from behind, nibbled on her ear. I hadn't seen him since we arrived yesterday. I had never heard him come in the night before, and Roni, Alyssa and I had been up pretty late—talking about everything under the sun—at least until three o'clock in the morning. By the time my eyes had begun to flutter, Grant still hadn't been home. Maybe he worked nights, I thought as I took a seat at the kitchen table, between Jason and Alyssa. Or maybe he just didn't want to stay at Grandpa Drew's house with the rest of us.

Mommy and Aunt Annette began making plates for the little ones, Nick and Nate. Jason was already scoffing down a plate of bacon, eggs and muffins. He barely even looked up. Just as Aunt Annette placed a plate in front of me, Roni walked into the kitchen, rubbed sleep from her eyes. She frowned at the sight of her mother and Grant at the kitchen sink together.

"Mom, have you seen my pink polo?" she asked Aunt Helen.

Aunt Helen turned to face the rest of us. She was actually blushing. "Uh, no, I haven't seen your pink polo, Roni. Have you looked in the laundry room?"

"It should've been washed with my other polos. They were all together," Roni insisted. It seemed that her goal was to get her mother's attention off Grant and on her at any cost.

"Well, I'm sorry. I haven't seen it," Aunt Helen said, "but I'll help you find it after we eat breakfast. Now have a seat."

Roni plopped down in the chair across from me. She sighed from frustration.

"I hate it when I can't find my things." Roni folded her arms across her chest. "They're never where they're supposed to be."

"You can wear my pink polo," I offered. "At least until you find yours."

"No thanks. I have my own," Roni said and then poured herself a glass of orange juice. "Can't wait until I'm grown and out of this house."

"Your mom doesn't need the attitude, Roni," Grant said, stuffing a piece of bacon into his mouth and heading for the front door.

"How would you know what my mom needs when you're never here?" Roni mumbled under her breath.

"Roni! You will mind your manners," Aunt Helen said and then headed for the front door to say goodbye to Grant.

"I can't stand him," Roni said after she was gone. "And I can't stand the way she puts him on a pedestal, like he's really something."

There was silence at the table for a moment.

"Well, baby, that's your mama's husband," Mommy replied, stepping in. "And you have to respect him, because he's also an adult."

"But, Aunt Mel, you don't understand. He doesn't even love her. He treats her so bad, yet she always puts him before me and Jason," Roni insisted. "Doesn't she, Jason?"

Everyone looked at Jason, waited for his response. He shrugged. "I don't really care, Roni," he finally said, "and you should stop trippin' about it, too."

Aunt Annette placed a plate of food in front of Roni. Roni began to eat in silence at first. And then she mumbled, "Nobody really understands."

"We can try and understand, sweetie," Mommy said. "You want to talk about it?"

"No. It doesn't really matter, Aunt Mel," Roni replied, then stuffed eggs into her mouth and shrugged. "It won't change anything."

We strolled through the mall, Roni, Alyssa and I, all three of us wearing Ecko Red jeans and similar tops. The moment Mommy's SUV had pulled up in front of Belk department store, Jason had made a beeline for the door. He wanted to be as far away from us as he possibly could. He wasn't interested in spending the day with three giggling girls, and we didn't really want to spend the day with him, either. It was better that way.

"I'll be back at two," Mommy had said. "Meet me right here in front of Belk."

I'd checked my watch and nodded a yes as she pulled out of the parking lot. It was nice to see so much eye candy on a Saturday afternoon. Lots of boys strolled through the hallways of the mall, either chatting on their cell phones or hanging out with their friends. Not that I was looking, but it was definitely a nice view.

We popped into Charlotte Russe and checked out their

clearance rack. Forever 21 was also having a sale, and I picked up a couple of new tops with the allowance that I'd earned just before we left Atlanta.

"I gotta go to the bathroom," I announced to my cousins as we approached Macy's.

"Yeah, I need to go, too," Alyssa said.

"Well, why don't we just make a group visit?" Roni said.

In the restroom's handicapped stall, I checked for my visitor again. No sign of it. It was at that point that I started to panic. My heart was pounding out of control; I wondered if my cousins could hear my heartbeat through the walls. I could hear it loud and clear. It seemed that it echoed through the restroom, bouncing off the walls, and every customer in the mall could hear it. Could it really be that I was pregnant? A missed menstrual cycle was usually the first sign. Pregnant at sixteen, just like my mother? No way! It could never happen to me. I was too smart, and besides, Vance and I had taken precautions.

I was in a daze as I sat there on the toilet. I stared at the salmon-colored door, where my leather jacket, my Forever 21 bag and my purse hung. I looked down at my sneakers and went through all the what-ifs. What if I was pregnant? How soon would I begin to show it? How would I tell my parents—especially my mother, who preached abstinence to me on a regular basis? What if they put me out on the street? Where would I go? How would I support myself? How would I tell Vance when he was on a fast track to play ball in college? What if he dumped me? And then there was Aunt Helen, who already thought that I was the fastest thing on the face of the earth. Would she ban me from the family once and for all? How would I support a child, with no job and no money?

"I'm trippin'," I whispered; at least I thought I was whispering.

Roni's voice rang out from the other side of the door. "Yes, you are trippin'! Can we go already?"

I stepped out of the stall, and Roni and Alyssa were waiting patiently. I couldn't even remember how long I'd been inside. I stepped up to the mirror, looked at my face. Looked at my stomach and the rest of my body, searching for a sign—anything.

"What is your problem, girl?" Roni asked.

"Are you okay, Tameka? You look like you've seen a ghost," Alyssa acknowledged.

Something was wrong, and I needed to handle it.

"I'm late," I said, turning on the faucet and holding my hands underneath the water.

"Late for what?" Roni asked. "You are acting way too strange for me."

"No, my cycle is late," I explained.

They both stared at me blankly.

"That doesn't mean anything," Alyssa said. "My cycle changes all the time. Sometimes it comes the first week of the month, sometimes two weeks later. We're athletes. That's not unusual."

"You don't understand," I told them. "Mine comes every month at the same time, like clockwork. Ever since I was twelve years old. It never changes."

When a white-haired older lady walked in, she smiled at us, and we lowered our voices to whispers.

"Well, how late are you?" Roni whispered.

"Today makes eight days," I said.

"Wow, and you're never late?" Alyssa asked.

"Never." I dried my hands on a paper towel, put my leather jacket on.

"You have to find out for sure," Roni said.

"How?" I asked.

"Follow me," Roni said.

Alyssa and I followed Roni out of the restroom, up the escalator at Macy's and outside. The wind was brisk, and I zipped my leather jacket all the way up.

"Where are we going?" I asked.

"Across the street," Roni responded.

We jaywalked across the busy street, right into the middle of mall traffic. A man driving a huge truck blew his horn as he'd just missed hitting us.

"Well, this is one way to handle the situation.... Why don't I just get myself killed?" I asked sarcastically and continued to follow Roni to the other side of the street and through the automatic doors at Walgreens.

We walked briskly past a clerk who was placing things on a shelf.

"Can I help you ladies find something?" she asked.

"No, thank you," I responded nervously.

I assumed that Roni knew exactly what she was looking for, as she led us straight for the aisle where the boxes of pregnancy tests were stacked on the shelves. She stood in front of them, scanned them one by one with her eyes.

"Here it is," she said and handed me a bright pink box with First Response across the front of it. "This is the best one."

"And how would you know that?" I asked, my hands on my hips and my eyebrows raised.

"Yeah." Alyssa wanted to know, too. "How do you know that?"

"I just know," Roni said.

"You been holding out on us," I said. "You been having sex!"

She didn't admit or deny it. She simply said, "It costs eighteen ninety-nine."

"I don't have that kind of cash! I just spent all I had at Forever 21," I said.

"Don't look at me," Alyssa said. "I'm flat broke."

"Fine," Roni said and snatched the pregnancy test from me. After checking the ceiling for cameras and mirrors, she opened the box, took out its contents and stuck them inside her jacket. She placed the empty box behind the other boxes on the shelf and said, "Let's go."

We walked quickly toward the door, trying to look inconspicuous. My heart pounded out of control.

"Did you ladies find what you needed?" asked a clerk.

"Yes, thank you," Alyssa responded for the group.

We walked right through the automatic doors, and no alarm went off. I exhaled as we stepped outside into the cold. We made our way across the busy street again and back to the mall, where we had ten minutes to spare before Mommy would pick us up.

"We got ten minutes. You wanna do it here?" Roni asked.

"No, not at the mall!" I exclaimed.

"Then where? At the house, with barracuda lady breathing down our throats?" Roni asked.

"I'd rather do it at home. We'll be really careful, and we'll dispose of the evidence."

"Cool," Roni said. "Let's go look for my juvenile delinquent brother."

As Mommy bounced to the sound of music, I watched her sadly from the backseat. She was so cool. People wished that my mom was their mom. She was my best friend in the whole world. I told her everything—we had no secrets. But suddenly, I had secrets that I couldn't tell my mom. At least not yet. I sang along with Beyoncé and looked out the window. Hoped for better days.

twenty-four

Indigo

LIFe was lonely without a cell phone. It was like you were on a deserted island, similar to the one that Tom Hanks was on in that movie *Cast Away*. It was a lonely place, and I was tempted to start talking to myself during the downtime. Other times, Mama was calling me to do the dishes or to clean up something. I hated that it was a Saturday. At least during the week I got to see my friends at school and talk to them. Once I got home, it was a different story.

Marcus had acted as if my fight with Jade was all my fault.

"I can't believe you, Indi. Fighting with your best friend," he'd said, slamming our locker shut—the one that we shared on the third floor of our school. "And at Macy's? For real? You don't have any shame, do you, Indigo Summer?"

"You act as if I was the only one fighting! Shouldn't she take some of the blame, too?" I'd asked.

"What is it with you and this spot on the team? Why can't you just let it go?"

Neither of us had answered the other's questions, and the entire conversation had become frustrating.

"I just felt like it should've been my spot, that's all."

"Then it sounds like your beef should be with Miss Martin. Not with Jade," Marcus said as we had stood in front of my classroom. "I'll see you after practice. You want me to come over to your house and study, or you comin' to mine?"

I shook my head no.

"What do you mean no?"

"We can't study together anymore. At least not until I get off punishment," I'd explained.

"Are you for real?" he'd asked. Nothing seemed to shock him at this point.

"Daddy's helping me with my math."

"Wow, you really messed up this time, Indi. Mr. Summer is helping with your math. You won't survive algebra." He'd laughed. "I'm sure it's been a thousand years since he had an algebra class."

"It's not funny."

"I'm not laughing at you." He'd smiled. "I'm laughing with you."

"Well, I'm not laughing."

"You have to admit that it is pretty funny when you think about it," Marcus had said. "But it's okay. You'll survive it." He'd walked backward down the hallway and then yelled, "I'll put some money on your books."

I'd stood there watching him for a few minutes, with his baggy black jeans sagging a little and his green Boston Celtics jersey with Pierce embroidered across the back. When I could no longer see him among the crowd in the hallway, I'd gone inside my classroom.

It had seemed like the longest school day ever.

Lying flat on my back and staring at the ceiling in my room was about all I had on my agenda for the day. Besides watching *Girlfriends* reruns back to back, staring at the ceiling was the most exciting part of my day. When I heard the light taps on my bedroom window, I knew it was Marcus. *Tap tap.* Sounded like he was throwing Skittles against the pane. I got up, opened the blinds. Marcus stood in his window—shirtless, with biceps, triceps and abs staring back at me. The elastic of his blue nylon shorts hung just below his six-pack.

"What's up?" he asked.

"Nothin'." I wasn't enthused at all.

"What you doing?"

"What do you think I'm doing? I'm grounded, Marcus," I said.

"Staring at the ceiling again?" He laughed.

"Not funny." I lowered my voice. Didn't want my parents hearing me talk to Marcus—they might nail my windows shut.

"Think you can sneak out later and meet me at the creek?" he asked.

"Are you asking me to break the rules, Marcus Carter?" I asked.

"I just miss you. I can't hold you at school like I want to, and since we can't study together anymore…well, you know…I just need to see you," he said.

"I need to see you, too," I admitted. "I'll meet you there at ten o'clock. I should be able to sneak out after Daddy goes to bed."

"Cool. I'll see you then." He pulled a Nike shirt over his head.

"Where you going now?" I asked, jealous because he was free and I was still a prisoner in my own home.

"Going over to the YMCA with Terrence to shoot some hoops," he said as he slipped a pair of sweats on over his shorts.

"Think of me while you're out there running free," I said dryly. "Can you bring me a Big Mac from Mickey D's?"

"I'll see what I can do." He slipped a gray hoodie on over his head. "I'll see you later on tonight. Be on time."

"Yeah, like I got so much to do in between now and then. That'll be the highlight of my day."

Marcus blew me a kiss and then vanished from the window.

Getting out of the house at ten o'clock wasn't going to be an easy task, but I was up for the challenge.

My parents' bedroom door was cracked just a little, the light from the television shining through the crack. I tiptoed past their room, my heart beating out of control. I could hear the newscaster on my parents' television giving the latest weather forecast. Daddy's snores echoed from the room as I crept down the stairs. When I made it to the front door, I twisted the lock and then turned the knob gently, pulled the door open. It creaked just a little bit, and it was just a few moments before I was on the other side, shivering from the cold. Wearing my pajamas, big fuzzy slippers and a winter coat, I headed for the creek behind our house—a place where Marcus and I met often. It was a place where we went to get away from the rest of the world, discuss our future. It was the place where I first became Marcus's girl. It was where he kissed me for the first time. It was a very special place.

He was already there, seated on a huge rock, a hoodie covering his head. A McDonald's bag in his hand, he waited patiently for me. He grinned when he saw me approaching.

"About time," he said, standing. "I was about to leave."

"I had to take my time." I fell into Marcus's arms. "You know I had to wait until Daddy was asleep."

As he hugged me strongly, his cologne tickling my nose, his cold lips touched mine. He lifted me off the ground and twirled me around in the air.

"I missed you, girl," he whispered.

I squeezed his neck. Wished we could stay like that forever. Even after my feet hit the ground again, I felt like I was still flying.

"Got my Big Mac?" I asked, grabbing for the bag.

"Of course," he said and pulled me onto his lap as he plopped down on the huge rock.

I opened the bag, opened the carton and eliminated the hamburger with just a few bites.

"You didn't want any, did you?" I asked once it was gone.

"Too late now." He laughed. "You greedy."

"You greedy!" I pushed Marcus, and he was so solid that he didn't even budge.

As I sat on Marcus's lap, he held me tightly around the waist. I wondered if our relationship would survive this punishment of mine. Wondered if Marcus would get bored or tired of waiting. Boys were like that. They were the most impatient people on the face of the earth. He never pressured me about sex or anything like that. In fact, I was the one who had pressured him about it when I was in the ninth grade. He'd thought it was too soon for us to even consider it. And we never really discussed it anymore. We had just sort of left it at that.

But the truth was, Marcus was getting older. He was becoming a man a lot faster than I was becoming a woman, and I wondered if he thought about it now. I wondered if he would step outside of our relationship, especially since I was on punishment indefinitely.

"Do you ever, you know, wanna holler at other girls?" I asked.

"What do you mean?" he asked.

"I mean, now that I'm on punishment, do you think about hooking up with somebody who's not on punishment?"

"Indi, that's silly. You won't be on punishment forever," he said.

"I know, but you might get bored with our relationship not going anywhere," I said, my eyes now looking right into his. "And I know girls who literally throw themselves at ballplayers."

"I'm a different kind of brother," he explained. "You know that."

"What about that girl, Raina, that you met in Houston last summer?" I asked.

"Her name was Rena," he said, correcting me. "And if you remember correctly, that whole pact idea was yours. 'Marcus, let's break up for the summer. That way if we meet somebody else, we can hook up with them…no pressure. Blah, blah, blah.' That was your idea, not mine."

"Tell me again, Marcus. Did you sleep with her?"

"Of course not, Indi. Now we said that we wouldn't talk about that stuff anymore," he said. "It's just me and you, remember?"

"I know, but this whole punishment thing's got me trippin'," I explained.

"Then do the right thing, Indi. And I'm sure you know what that is," he said. "And as for me, I'm not going anywhere. I don't care if you're on punishment for the rest of the school year. I'll be here waiting to spend the summer with you."

His smile was so beautiful. It was his best physical attribute, but there was so much more to Marcus than the physical. He was sweet. Sometimes I wondered if I really deserved him.

"Thank you, Marcus," I whispered and kissed his lips.

"You won't be grounded forever, Indi. Just quit being a wimp about it." He smiled.

"I'm not being a wimp."

"Yes, you are. But you're a girl, so it's okay," he said. "Now come on, girl. Let's get you back in the house before the warden sends out the dogs."

He grabbed my hand and led the way back to the front of my house.

"You go on ahead. I have to do this like Rambo or 007. I need some time," I told him.

"Cool." He kissed my forehead. "I'll see you tomorrow at school."

"Okay," I whispered, sad to see him go. I shivered as I watched him stroll to the front of his house, go up the stairs and cross his front porch.

He vanished, and I stood on the side of my house, my back against the wall as my heart pounded again. I crept up the front stairs and onto the porch. I turned the doorknob, oh, so carefully. The door creaked again as I entered the foyer in my house. Creeping up the stairs again, I stood still when I heard a noise. It was just Daddy's snoring again. I crept past my parents' room and slipped into my room. Pulled my coat and slippers off, hopped into bed. My heart was still pounding.

It had been dangerous, but well worth it.

twenty-five

Tameka

cramped in the small bathroom, with the door locked, the three of us stood awaiting the results of my pregnancy test. My heart pounded as a faint little plus sign appeared on the stick. It was positive. According to the stolen pregnancy test, I was definitely pregnant. The three of us stared at each other in disbelief.

"How accurate are these things?" I asked. Something had to be wrong, I thought.

"They're, like, ninety-nine point nine percent accurate," Roni said.

"Oh my God, Tameka. What are you gonna do?" Alyssa asked.

I sat on the toilet with the lid down. "I don't know. I guess I was expecting it to be negative. I hadn't really thought past that part."

"I thought you and Vance used protection," Alyssa said.

"We did." I was a little dazed and suddenly felt sick. "I swear we did."

"Condoms aren't a one hundred percent guarantee, you

know. You can still get pregnant even when you use them." Roni acted as if she was an expert on the matter. "The best way to prevent pregnancy and HIV is to not do it at all."

"Yeah, but the percentage is, like, ninety-nine percent," I argued.

"But it's not a hundred. And that one percent is what got you messed up." Roni shrugged. "I guess you better start saving your allowance for Pampers and formula."

"Not funny." I couldn't breathe. "I need some air." I opened the small bathroom window.

"Will you keep it, Tameka?" Alyssa asked.

"I don't know." I covered my face with the palms of my hands. My mind raced a million miles a minute. Thousands of thoughts, but none of them made sense.

I jumped when someone pounded on the door.

"I gotta use it!" Nick whined. "Let me pee!"

Roni scrambled to collect our evidence, the pregnancy test paraphernalia. She placed everything into a brown paper bag and stuffed the bag into the pocket of her hoodie. Once everything was cleaned up, she said, "Open the door."

Alyssa opened the door, and the three of us stepped out into the hallway. Nick rushed past us and slammed the door behind him. We made a beeline for the pink room, where I plopped down on the bed. Tears streamed down the sides of my face. My cousins sat down on each side of me; they cried, too. That was all we knew to do at that moment.

"Don't cry," Alyssa said. "We'll come up with something."

"Something like what?" I asked. "You got a magic wand somewhere? Can you reverse the results of that pregnancy test?"

Alyssa just shook her head. There was nothing that any of us could do.

"I had an abortion once," Roni said.

Alyssa and I both looked at Roni. Shocked.

"Really. When?" I asked.

"A year ago," Roni said.

"You were pregnant a year ago, and you never told us!" Alyssa said.

"I hated the person that I was pregnant by." Roni looked straight ahead, a strange blank look on her face. "I was pretty much raped."

"Who was it?" I asked. "Do you know?"

Roni sighed. "Remember when I said that now that Grandpa Drew is gone, he can't protect me anymore? Not from the barracuda lady, and not from Lucifer?"

"Well, we all know who the barracuda lady is," I said.

"But who is Lucifer?" Alyssa asked.

Roni sat quietly for a moment, a deep frown on her face. "Grant," she said. "Grant is Lucifer."

"I don't get it," Alyssa said.

"Grant raped you, didn't he?" I asked. I understood it. That was why she hated him so much. I saw it in her eyes at the breakfast table, and every time she spoke his name.

"He makes me wanna throw up," Roni mumbled through clenched teeth. "He just does it whenever he wants to."

"You mean he's done it more than once?" I asked.

"He used to," Roni said. "Until I finally told Grandpa Drew what was going on."

"What did he say?" I asked.

"He pointed his shotgun right between Grant's eyes one night and told him that he would blow him to kingdom come if he put one finger on me again." Tears were streaming down Roni's face. "But now Grandpa Drew's gone, and I'm all alone."

"You have to tell your mom," I urged.

Roni looked at me as if I'd just said the most ridiculous thing in the world.

"Do you think she doesn't know?" Roni asked.

"She knows?" Alyssa asked.

"Who do you think took me to the abortion clinic?" Roni asked.

Was she kidding? Aunt Helen knew about all of this? I kept waiting for Roni to say that it was all a lie, that she was just telling one of her sick, twisted jokes.

"Are you telling me that Aunt Helen knew about this, and she's still with him?" I had to get a clear understanding of this. It was the most unbelievable thing I'd ever heard. It was absurd.

"Grandpa Drew told her that if she didn't handle this situation, he was gonna handle it for her," Roni said. "You wanna know how she handled it? She sent me to your house in Atlanta for two weeks. When I came back, nobody ever talked about it again. It was as if it never happened, as if it was just a figment of my imagination. That's how it was handled."

"I'm so sorry that happened to you, Roni," I said. "I never really liked Grant in the first place, but I hate him even more now."

"You know what he said the night that Grandpa Drew passed away?" Roni asked.

"What?" Alyssa was on the edge of the bed.

"'Who's gonna protect you now?' That's what he asked me," Roni said.

"Sick bastard," I mumbled. I never used that type of language, but I was angry. I wanted to hurt Grant the way he'd hurt my cousin. But I felt helpless. If her own mother wouldn't help, then who would?

"We have to do something," Alyssa said.

"You can't tell Uncle Rich or Uncle Paul," Roni pleaded. "It'll only make things worse for me here. After you're all gone, he'll punish me."

"Well, we have to do something, Roni," I said.

"You have your own worries," Roni said. "What are you gonna do about your problem?" She pointed toward my stomach.

She was right. I did have worries. In the midst of everything, I'd already forgotten about them. But now the reality of my situation slapped me in the face again. I was going to either have an abortion at sixteen or be a mother at sixteen, and either choice was a huge one. Each choice had its consequences. Each choice would change my life forever.

The three of us held on to each other tightly. We all knew that things would never be the same.

twenty-six

Vance

I stared at the white envelope, and it stared back at me. My mother had slipped it into my room and laid it facedown on my dresser. The return address said Grambling State University. I had applied without my father's knowledge. In his mind, I didn't need to apply anywhere but Duke. But my mother knew what I wanted. She knew that I wanted to explore my options and had encouraged me to do just that.

"Go ahead and apply to other schools," she'd said. "This is your future. Your father has lived his life."

"It's hard to tell him that, though," I'd tried to explain.

"You apply, and if you're accepted, I'll handle your father for you," she'd promised.

I slipped my finger inside the curve of the envelope, opened it carefully and unfolded the letter.

"We are pleased to notify you that you have been accepted to Grambling State University...." I read the words softly. "A four-year full scholarship. Room and board..."

I sat on the edge of my bed. Read through the letter

again, until I heard a light tap on the door. Mom stuck her head in.

"Can I come in?" she asked.

"Yeah," I whispered. "Check this out."

I handed her the letter, and she took a seat on the bed, next to me. Read it silently.

"Oh, baby. This is so good." She smiled. "They're offering you a free ride."

"I know," I said. "But it's too bad I can't take it."

"Why can't you?" she asked. "I told you I would handle your father."

"He's had my life planned for me since I was five. I'm supposed to graduate from Duke on a full scholarship and go on to medical school. Become a dentist like him."

"I thought you wanted to go to law school," she said.

"I do."

"Then that's where you'll be going. This is your life, not your father's." She kissed my cheek. "Congratulations, son. You did it, and I'm proud of you."

"Thanks, Ma."

"Now get cleaned up for dinner," she said. "I'll talk to your father later."

At the dinner table, the conversation was the same as usual. Dad talked about the clients he had serviced during the course of the day, discussed how many teeth he'd pulled, how many root canals he'd performed and how many people's teeth were the worst he'd ever seen in his life. He had seen so many cavities in his life, it wasn't even funny. Lori talked about her day at school and how much more money she needed for cheerleading. It seemed the cheerleaders were always asking for money for this and money for that. Dad would just write a check for whatever it was. Mom talked about her latest court case. She was representing a man who'd been accused of murdering his wife. It was intriguing to listen to her courtroom stories. Made me want to be just like her.

My day had been pretty boring, and so I did not have much to contribute to the dinner conversation. Unable to play basketball because of my injury, I usually sat out at practices and games.

"Honey, guess what happened to Vance today?" Mom began.

"What?" Dad asked.

"He got an acceptance letter from Grambling," she said. "He got a full ride, a spot on the team… Doesn't get much better than that."

"Really? That's all right, son." Dad smiled. "I told you scouts were watching you."

"Yep." I looked at Mom. Wondered where she was going with this conversation.

"I'm so proud of him. He loves that school," Mom continued.

"I'm proud of him, too. Just goes to show what a good ballplayer he is," Dad said. "Duke will be lucky to have him."

"Honey, he's thinking seriously about Grambling," Mom said. "That's where he wants to go."

"Babe, we've been through this before. He's not going to Grambling," Dad said. "They don't have anything to offer him. Duke is a good undergraduate school, and they have a decent premed program."

"That's another thing," Mom began. They spoke about me in third person, as if I wasn't even in the room. "He's not interested in medical school, baby."

"What?" Dad smiled, as if what my mother had said was ludicrous. "Are you kidding? This boy's been groomed for dentistry since he was a little boy. Look at his hands. He's got the fingers of a dentist. I bet you he can tell you right now how to perform a root canal. Can't you, son?"

"Yes, sir," I confessed. I had watched my father perform root canals a million times. I knew exactly how to prep a patient.

I knew every step, and even though I didn't have a degree, I knew how to perform a root canal better than any dentist, any day of the week.

"You see, babe, he's a doctor at heart."

"He really isn't," Mom said. "And if you really took the time to listen to your son, you would know that his love is for the law."

Dad laughed and then looked my way, as if he expected me to laugh, too. I wasn't laughing at all.

"Vance, what is your mother talking about?" he asked.

"She, uh...well, see..." I stumbled over my words. Why was I so nervous? "I've gone to the office with Mom a few times, and to the courtroom, too. Man! The courtroom is just so interesting to me. It's an awesome place, for real. And seeing Mom work her magic and all...I just can't even describe it. She's a genius, Dad. You should see her...."

He was looking at me as if I'd lost my mind.

"Man, there's so much I could do with a law degree. I could be a lawyer. I could go on to be a judge. Wearing that fly robe and bangin' my gavel and throwing the book at criminals." Verbalizing my desires to my dad had me excited. "I could become a senator or the United States attorney general."

Mom was smiling. Dad looked as if he'd seen a ghost. I was waiting for him to throw something across the table, knock me in the head with it.

"Wow," he said softly. "I didn't know you felt like that."

"It's not that I don't like dentistry, Dad. I think what you do is cool, but law is really where my heart is."

"I can respect that," Dad said. "I want you to succeed at whatever you decide to do, son."

"I think I will do a better job with my studies at a school where I'm comfortable." I just went for it. "I feel like I would be more successful academically at Grambling than I would at Duke."

"That's not possible, son," Dad said. "There's no comparison between the two schools. I attended Duke. Your grandfather attended Duke. All my friends and colleagues are administrators there. You have a sure shot for success."

"That's exactly what I'm talking about. All of your college buddies are there. I would never feel like I was succeeding on my own," I said. "They would be breathing down my neck all the time."

"Is that what this is all about? My colleagues breathing down your neck?" He sighed. "You don't have a clue about what's best for you."

"I really do, Dad. And I'm going to Grambling," I stated matter-of-factly.

Silence filled the room. I had taken a risk, stepping out there, standing up to my father for the first time in my life. I knew that he loved me and only wanted what was best for me, but I was standing firm in my decision. He wasn't having to fork over any cash for my education. Either way, I was getting a free ride, so what difference did it make to him where I spent the next four years of my life? Both Duke and Grambling were good schools, and I wanted Grambling.

"Is that your final choice?" he asked.

"Yes, sir," I replied.

I waited for him to send me to my room—take away all my privileges until I came to my senses.

"Then I guess you're going to Grambling," he said.

He was hurt. It was written all over his face. Disappointment filled his entire being. But what could he say? I would be eighteen in just a few weeks and could make my own decisions.

"Can I be excused?" I asked.

"Of course," Dad said and motioned for me to leave the table.

I went upstairs to my room, shut the door behind me. I pulled my Grambling State T-shirt out of my drawer, shook it in order to knock the wrinkles out. I pulled it over my head, checked it out in the mirror.

I looked good in gold and black.

twenty–seven

Tameka

TWO long, sleek black town cars pulled up in front of Grandpa Drew's house. The cars seemed to make it all real. The boys were dressed in their gray, brown and black suits. Alyssa wore a black dress with black panty hose and her sexy Nine West shoes. Roni wore a two-piece gray pantsuit and a pair of gray pumps. I had chosen my red dress because it was the only thing I'd packed that offered the room that I needed to hide my stomach. Although my stomach hadn't started growing yet, I was still paranoid. The last thing I needed was for someone to notice that I'd picked up a few pounds or had a little pouch in my midsection. I chose my black tights because they offered that extra support that I needed in the stomach area.

I held on to Mommy's hand as we sat on the sofa in the living room. My heart was beating faster than a freight train.

"The cars are here," Uncle Rich announced.

Aunt Helen rushed outside to meet the drivers, probably to give them last-minute instructions about how she wanted things to go. She loved giving orders, especially during this time.

I looked at Aunt Helen differently now. She had never been my favorite person, but now I had absolutely no respect for her. She had allowed Roni to be violated in the worst way and hadn't done a thing about it. I was angry with her.

As we all slipped our winter coats on, Daddy grabbed my hand. He gave me a warm smile, and I gave him one back.

"You ready?" he asked.

"Not really, but I don't have a choice," I said.

At the church, soft music played in the background as we sat in front of Grandpa Drew's casket. He looked as if he were sleeping, lying there in his gray pin-striped suit and wearing the same burgundy tie that he'd worn to Aunt Helen's wedding. His brown, ashy-looking hands were folded on top of his chest. His gray hair and mustache were trimmed perfectly, and somehow a little smile twinkled in the corner of his mouth. Grandpa Drew had been a Christian, so I knew that he had already gone to Heaven. The body that lay motionless in front of us was not really him—not anymore; it was just a shell that he'd used while he was here on earth. I knew that he was there, though. In the church somewhere, he was looking down on us and smiling. Probably nudging one of his newfound buddies in Heaven, telling him one of his corny jokes.

I imagined he was probably disappointed with me. Probably frowning at the fact that I'd made such a stupid mistake and messed up my life.

"I thought you were the smart one in the bunch, ladybug," he'd say if he could.

"Everybody makes mistakes, Grandpa Drew," I would say in my defense.

"It's okay, though." Grandpa Drew had never held a grudge. He'd disciplined with love, but made sure that every one of us knew that he cared. "I still love you," Grandpa Drew would tell me. He would hold me tight, and I would know that everything would be all right.

Uncle Rich was the vocalist in our family, and at the front of the church, he sang a solo. He barely made it through before tears filled his light brown eyes, and before long the entire congregation was crying. The pastor of the church gave our family words of comfort. Aunt Helen, Aunt Beverly, Daddy and a few of Grandpa Drew's friends gave short little speeches in remembrance of my grandfather.

At the end of the service, we each had one last opportunity to look at Grandpa Drew before they closed the casket. Everyone went forward one by one in order to bid farewell to a good man. Grant held on to Aunt Helen when her legs became frail. She was crying and screaming out of control, and I wondered what all the screaming was about. It was Roni who should've been screaming the loudest. She would be the one suffering the most after we all went back home.

"I'll see you in my dreams," I whispered to Grandpa Drew while the choir sang another selection.

I could've sworn I heard him say, "I'll be there, ladybug."

I wondered if he would be there when I told my parents that I was pregnant. I hoped so, because I would need all the moral support I could get.

Grandpa Drew's house was filled with lots of people. Some of them were members of our family, while others were members of his church. A few of them were neighbors and friends, who brought fried chicken, macaroni and cheese, sweet-potato pies and other desserts. There was so much food, and it seemed to just keep coming.

Roni, Alyssa and I quickly changed out of our dress clothes and into more comfortable ones. We sat in our pink bedroom and talked about everyone. We laughed at how the choir had sung every song off-key, and how Roni had dozed when the pastor started giving his words of comfort. We all agreed that Uncle Rich's solo had been the best part of the service.

"I swear to God, that big lady in the choir had the hots for Grandpa Drew," Roni said.

"The one in the floral dress?" Alyssa said.

"Yes." Roni laughed. "She was crying like she'd lost a husband, and I thought she was gonna climb into the casket with him."

"I saw her," I said, remembering the woman with white hair and big breasts.

"She's been over here before," Roni said. "She was always bringing cookies and pies for Grandpa Drew. They even sat on the porch a few times, rocking and talking until the wee hours of the night."

"Yep, something was definitely going on between those two." I laughed. "Nobody was crying harder."

"Except for barracuda lady. I thought she was gonna blow a gasket," Roni said. "She should win an Academy Award. She and her sleazy husband."

"What are we going to do about him, by the way?" I asked. "We can't leave you here like that."

"There's nothing you can do," Roni said. "Besides, you got your own issues."

"When are you going to tell your parents, Tameka?" Alyssa asked.

I shrugged. I didn't have any answers.

"You'd better make some decisions fast," Roni said. "Especially if you decide to get an abortion. You have to do it before you get too far along. Otherwise, you're putting yourself in danger."

"I'll deal with it as soon as I get home," I told them. "Now, as for you, Roni, I think you should tell my mom your secret. Maybe she can help. Maybe she could arrange for you to come and live with us for a while."

"Won't ever happen. Barracuda lady's not going for that," Roni said.

"What won't ever happen?" My mom walked into the room, carrying her pumps in her hand. "My feet hurt."

"Hi, Aunt Mel." Alyssa smiled.

"Hello, girls." Mommy looked at each of us, one after the other, suspicion in her eyes. "What are you up to?"

"Nothing," Roni quickly answered.

"Tell her," I mumbled under my breath.

"Tell me what?" Mommy asked.

"Nothing. Your daughter's losing it," Roni said, playing it off.

I jumped right in there. "Roni wants to come and stay with us for a while."

"She does?" Mommy asked. "What about school?"

"She can go to school in Atlanta," I said. "We can enroll her in school. We can fix up the guest bedroom for her and everything."

"Why would she want to come to Atlanta, Tameka? Her mother is here in Charlotte," Mommy said.

I kept answering for Roni. "Because she hates her stepfather. He's a punk."

"Watch your language, girl," Mommy said. "I know you don't really care for Grant, Roni, but he is your mother's husband. He's the man that she chose to spend the rest of her life with, whether you like it or not."

"I know, Aunt Mel, but…" Roni's voice was beginning to crack.

"He did something bad to her, Aunt Mel," Alyssa interrupted. "Something that he should go to jail for."

My mother immediately shut the door and locked it. There was deep concern in her eyes.

"What is going on, Roni? You tell me right now what he did to you!" Mommy demanded.

Roni was silent. Tears began to creep down the sides of her face.

"He raped her," Alyssa whispered.

"More than once, too," I added.

"Is this true, Roni?" Mommy grabbed Roni's hands in hers, held them tight.

Roni shook her head yes.

"Oh my God, baby. I'm so sorry." Mommy grabbed Roni and held her. She rocked her and wouldn't let go. "That's why you hate him so much."

"You can't tell Uncle Paul or Uncle Rich," Roni pleaded. "They wouldn't understand."

"Does your mother know?" Mommy asked.

The looks on our faces told her that the answer was yes. My mother was furious; I could see it in her eyes.

"Please don't say anything, Aunt Mel. It will only make it worse," Roni pleaded.

"I will handle this," Mommy promised. "One way or another, I will handle this. Pack yourself a bag. You're going back to Atlanta with us."

"She won't let me go," Roni said.

"Oh, she'll let you go, or there will be hell to pay," Mommy warned. "You pack a bag, and I'll handle the rest."

"Thank you, Aunt Mel." Roni wrapped her arms around my mother's neck. "Thank you for protecting me now that Grandpa Drew is gone."

With a confused look on her face, Mommy stood and approached the door.

"Got any more secrets you want to share with me?" she asked.

My eyes bounced from Roni to Alyssa, and their eyes landed on me.

"Got any more secrets, Tameka?" Roni asked.

"Nope. That's it," I lied.

"Good. That's enough for one night." Mommy sighed. "People are finally starting to leave, and it'll be quiet around here soon. Tameka, start getting your things together. Your dad wants to pull out of here early in the morning."

"Okay, Mommy," I said. "I'll be ready."

She didn't say another word. She just left the room, shutting the door behind her. At least Roni's secret was out there, in the air, with a solution just around the corner. If anyone could handle things, it was my mother. She knew just how to make things right.

"You feel better?" I asked Roni.

"Much," Roni said. "Aunt Mel's cool."

"I told you," I said. "Everything will be just fine."

"What about you?" Roni asked. "How are you going to handle your little problem?"

"I'm not sure yet," I confessed.

It was true. I wasn't sure yet. All I knew was that I couldn't leave Roni in North Carolina to deal with her mother's husband all by herself. She wasn't strong enough to do it. I would deal with my problem once I got home. One way…or another.

twenty-eight

Indigo

The mediator in juvenile court thought that Jade and I could benefit from a few hours of community service. She thought it was a good idea that we spend forty hours at a homeless shelter for women and children. Why? I didn't know, but our parents thought it was a wonderful idea, too. The next four Saturdays and Sundays of our lives would be dedicated to working in a food kitchen, reading books to little homeless children and performing odd jobs as needed.

Plastic yellow gloves on my hands and a bandanna on my head, I swung the handle of the mop across the wooden floor in one swoop. The bathroom smelled like pee as I mopped the floor around the toilets. Jade, wearing similar plastic gloves, poured Pine-Sol onto the countertops and wiped them down with an old rag. After mopping and cleaning the bathrooms, we washed our hands and headed downstairs to the kitchen to serve lunch.

I tied an apron around my waist and stood behind the mashed potatoes. A plastic serving spoon in hand, I plopped mashed potatoes onto the plate of each person who passed through the line. Their faces looked so sad, especially those of the children. There were even a few teenagers who lived there with their mother, a family with no place else to go. I couldn't even imagine living in a place like that, and I felt sorry for them.

"Thank you," said a little girl with big brown eyes as I gave her a spoonful of mashed potatoes. "I like your hair, and you're very pretty."

"Thank you." I smiled. She was sweet.

This might not be so bad, after all, I thought. A few weeks of this wouldn't kill me. I helped clean up the kitchen, folded my apron and placed it on the countertop. Stood downstairs and waited for my daddy to pick me up. Jade did exactly the same thing, and we stood there in silence. We still weren't on speaking terms. I just wanted to get my forty hours done and get off punishment. That was my only goal. I missed Marcus like crazy, and I needed my cell phone like the children in Africa needed food.

"Thank you, ladies," said Maria, one of the counselors at the shelter. "I'll see you tomorrow. Maybe you can read to the children in the morning. I think they would really like that."

"You're welcome." Jade and I said it at the same time.

As soon as I got home, I rushed upstairs to my room, threw a Skittle at Marcus's window. I needed to see his face. When he didn't respond, I threw another one. A few minutes later, he raised his blinds.

"What took you so long?" I asked.

"I was in the shower." He smiled. With a towel wrapped around his waist, he brushed his waves. "So, how was it?"

"It was stupid!" I said. "Some of those people are so pitiful. I would never end up in a place like that."

"Never say never, Indi. You don't know where life will take you. You can't judge people like that," he said.

"It's a shelter for women and children. Some of the women are battered. Wouldn't you know that your husband was an abuser before you even hooked up with him?"

"Not necessarily," Marcus said. "Think about it, Indi. Remember when you hooked up with Quincy Rawlins? Did you know that he was a cheater?"

"No!" I said. What kind of question was that? "If I had known that, I wouldn't have hooked up with him in the first place."

"Exactly," Marcus said. "He made you believe that he was cool just so he could get into your pants. And even after I told you that he was no good, you still wanted to be with him."

"It's not the same," I said. "He never abused me. That's different."

"It's somewhat the same," he argued.

"But after I saw him at the movies with Patrice, I dropped him. I didn't keep going back to him, like a retard," I said. "These women keep going back, even after their husbands nearly kill them."

"So what? People do crazy stuff for love," Marcus said. "You can't judge people, Indi."

"I'm not judging anybody. I'm just saying, I wouldn't end up like them." I stood firm.

Marcus decided to change the subject. Sometimes we had to agree to disagree. "What're you about to do?"

"Clean up the kitchen and then start on my science project," I told him. "What about you?"

"Me and Terrence are going to the mall later."

I was jealous of Marcus's freedom. I couldn't wait until I was free, too. This being grounded thing was starting to get old—fast. However, I could see a light at the end of the tunnel. I had to stay on task and make sure I walked a straight walk. It wasn't all bad. Recently I'd turned in more homework assignments than I had all year, and I'd learned that Daddy actually knew more about algebra than I'd thought he did. He wasn't a bad tutor, after all. I missed my cell phone and my social life, though, and my handsome boyfriend, who was busy having a life without me.

"Cool. Have fun," I said sadly.

"Keep your head up, beautiful," Marcus said. "It won't be long."

"It seems like forever since we hung out," I whined.

"Be patient. I'll be right here waiting when you get out of jail." He smiled.

"You better," I insisted.

"I'll even bring you something back from the mall," he said. "What do you want?"

"Can you just bring me a Big Mac from McDonald's?"

"I'll see what I can do, Madam Inmate," he teased. "Now get that science project started, and I'll see you later."

"The usual place?" I asked.

"Same place, same time," Marcus said, referring to our creek in the backyard, "and don't be late, Indi. I'm not playing."

"I'll be on time," I insisted, and before he could reply, I shut the window and stuck out my tongue.

I would be counting down the minutes until I saw him again.

Sunday after church, it was back to the grind again. The children at the homeless shelter gathered around me in a circle on the floor. Dr. Seuss's book *The 500 Hats of Bartholomew Cubbins* in my hand, I read to them, and they giggled when I got to the funny parts. I rushed through the ending and shut the book, letting Jade take over with her book. She read them a different Dr. Seuss book, *The Cat in the Hat,* and they giggled like it was the first time they'd ever heard it. At the end of the story, they clapped, and it felt good. Who would've thought that a simple Dr. Seuss story would bring laughter to a bunch of little kids? I didn't think it was that serious, but obviously, it was to them.

Jade and I washed our hands and headed for the huge kitchen. We placed aprons around our waists and prepared to serve fried chicken, rice and green beans to the residents.

"I'm so glad that you girls are here," said a woman as she approached us. She looked as if she might've been pretty at one time in her life. But her eyes looked worn, and she just looked tired. Her hands were burned, and I wondered if her abusive husband had had anything to do with it. "My daughter used to be just like you. A normal teenager."

Jade and I gave each other a puzzled look. A young girl who looked like she was about fifteen or sixteen approached the woman. The woman wrapped her arm around the girl's frail body. Her eyes were so sad.

"I'm Rita," the woman said. "And this is my daughter, Jamina. We've been here for about three weeks now. This is our fourth shelter in two months. Looking at you two gives me such hope for Jamina. I can't wait until she's back to being a normal teenager again. She hasn't been in a long time."

I wanted to ask her what happened. I wanted to know why Jamina wasn't normal anymore, but instead, I asked, "Would you like some fried chicken?"

"I want some of everything, sweetheart," Rita said. "What is your name?"

"Indigo," I said. "Indigo Summer."

"And yours?" She turned to Jade.

"I'm Jade Morgan."

"It's so nice to meet you both," Rita said and smiled. "Tell the girls hello, Jamina."

Jamina just looked at us with her sad eyes. Never mumbled a word. She was strange, and it was hard to believe that she had ever been normal like us. I slapped a spoonful of rice onto Rita's plate and then onto Jamina's, and was glad when they moved on so that I could serve the next person in line. I couldn't wait to get this day over with, get home and finish my homework. Maybe even catch a glimpse of Marcus in his bedroom window.

I felt sorry for Jamina, but unlike her, I had a life.

At the end of the afternoon, I sat next to Jade in the day area of the shelter, where we both waited for our parents to pick us up.

"Jamina was strange, huh?" I asked her. These were the first words that I had uttered to her since our fight at Macy's.

"Very," she said.

Honestly, I hadn't expected her to respond, but I exhaled when she did. I was glad to have a conversation with her again, even if it was just a few words. Although I would never admit it, I missed her. And somehow I could tell that she missed me, too.

"Uncle Ernest is here," I said when I saw her father pull up.

"Thanks," she said and zipped her coat up. "I'll see you."

I watched as my ex–best friend ran outside, hopped into the back of her daddy's SUV. Life was tricky sometimes.

twenty-nine

Tameka

RONI'S bags sat at the front door, right next to mine. She was already up, showered, dressed and ready to go. Her nerves were on edge, wondering how my mother was going to pull this off. I wondered, too. My mother wasn't Aunt Helen's favorite person, and I wondered how she was going to convince Aunt Helen to let her take her only daughter to Atlanta to live with us. I didn't see Aunt Helen agreeing to such a deal. But Mommy had promised that she'd handle it, so I had faith that she would.

"Are we ready to go, girls?" Mommy asked as we both came down the stairs.

Confused, we looked at each other and both answered, "Yes, ma'am."

Aunt Helen came out of the kitchen, carrying a cup of coffee. I braced myself for the confrontation that was about to take place.

"Did you pack your inhaler?" Aunt Helen asked Roni. "I know you haven't had an attack in a long time, but you never know."

It was no secret that Roni was prone to have an occasional

asthma attack. She'd just about grown out of it, but every now and then the asthma would flare up. Aunt Helen seemed agreeable to Roni going back with us, and I was shocked. What had my mother said to her?

"I got it in my bag," Roni said. She was just as shocked as I was. I could see it on her face.

"I'll load the bags into the car," Daddy called. He came out of the kitchen and picked up my overnight bag on wheels and Roni's, too. Took them to the car.

Aunt Helen grabbed Roni's face in her hands and said, "You're gonna finish the school year out in Atlanta with Tameka. You'll stay with Aunt Mel and Uncle Paul for a while, and when school's out, I'll send for you."

Roni nodded a yes.

"You already know to behave yourself, right?" Aunt Helen brushed her fingers through Roni's bangs on her forehead.

"Yes," replied Roni.

"Roni's never a problem at our house, Helen. She'll be just fine," Mommy said, with such confidence.

She had taken care of things just like she'd promised. But how? What had taken place between Mommy and Aunt Helen between last night and the crack of dawn this morning? And what was going to change by the time school was out in a few months?

Daddy came back in for the second round of bags and loaded them into the car. Roni and I went into the kitchen, pulled cereal bowls from the shelf and poured two bowls of Froot Loops. I grabbed the carton of milk out of the refrigerator and poured some into each bowl. I took a seat next to Roni at the breakfast table.

"What do you think happened?" I whispered.

"I don't know, but something's strange," Roni whispered. "She's not even trippin', like she normally does."

"I'm just glad you don't have to stay here," I told her.

"Me, too." She smiled and danced in her seat. "I'm going to the A."

"I can't wait to show you around my school," I told her. "It's too late for you to get on the dance team, but I'll introduce you to all my friends. They're cool."

She smiled. "I feel like I can breathe now. I don't know what Aunt Mel did, but I'm forever grateful. And I'm glad you told her. I was mad at you at first, but now I'm glad."

"Me, too." I stuffed a spoonful of Froot Loops into my mouth. "Now if I can just figure out a solution to my little issue."

"I got your back, Tameka. Whatever you decide, I'm there for you," she promised.

I smiled. I was grateful, because I was going to need all the help I could get for this one.

In the backseat of the car, Roni's head bounced against the window, her mouth wide open, with light snores escaping from her chafed lips. I nudged her just so she would stop storing. She sat up, looked around and then was at it again. I opened my cell phone. Sent Vance a text.

Good morning, I said.

Same 2 u.

On my way home.

Cool, he responded.

Missed u. It was true. I had.

Ditto, he texted back.

I wondered how he would feel about being a father. Wondered if he knew that his life was about to change drastically right before his eyes. It was just last night that I'd finally built up the nerve to tell Vance my news. I'd decided that I owed him at least the privilege of knowing the truth. It was the right time. I needed his input. We needed to make a decision together. I had waited until it was late, until everyone in the house was asleep and I could barely hear a peep. I had crept into the small bathroom, shut and locked the door behind me. Dialed Vance's number. It had rung three times before he finally picked up.

"What's up?" he'd asked.

"Were you sleep?" I had whispered, careful not to wake anyone in the house.

"A little bit," he'd said. "What's up?

"I just wanted to talk to you." I could've blurted it out right then. Could've told him about the life that was growing in my stomach, but I didn't. Instead, I'd beaten around the bush. "How was school today?"

"It was cool. The usual. Nothing special," he'd said. "You went to your grandfather's funeral?"

"Yeah. It was sad," I'd told him. "I tried calling you earlier. I had something I wanted to tell you."

"I wanted to call you earlier, too, but didn't know if it was a good time," he'd said. "I had something to tell you, too."

"What was it?"

"You go first," he'd offered.

"No, you go first," I'd said. "Mine can wait."

"Grambling offered me a scholarship." I could hear the smile in his voice. "Got my letter today."

"For real?" I was excited for him.

"Yeah, I even told my father that I wasn't going to med school. Told him that I wanted to be a lawyer."

"Really? How did he take it?"

"He rolled with it," Vance had said.

"That's cool, boo. I'm so happy for you!" It was the best news I'd heard all weekend.

"Yeah, I'm happy, too," he'd said. "Now what was your news?"

There was no way I could rain on his parade.

"Never mind," I said. "It's nothing compared to your news. I'm proud of you."

"Thank you," he'd said.

"Well, I gotta go. I'm sorry I woke you up. Hope you can go back to sleep," I'd said. "Text me if you can't."

"Okay, I will," he'd said. "Can't wait until you get home. I need to see you."

"I need to see you, too," I'd said. "Text me later. I'll wait up."

"Bye."

When I'd hung up the phone, I'd known that this was going to be much harder than I thought it would be. Vance needed to know, but the timing was definitely not right.

That was last night, and today was a new day. Today I would have to tell Vance the truth. He needed to know as soon as possible. I shut my phone and stuck it inside my Coach purse. Decided to join Roni in sleep land. With my head against the back of the leather seat, I shut my eyes. Hoped for sweeter dreams.

thirty

Tameka

RONI and I changed the sheets on the bed in the guest bedroom, even though I knew she would end up sleeping in the extra twin bed in my room. We still went through the motions. Whenever she stayed with us, she took the guest bedroom, but we always ended up talking until the wee hours of the morning, and she would just crash in my room. She headed for the shower, and I pulled out my cell phone. Dialed Vance's number. He had to be told once and for all. There was no way around it.

"You're home?" he said when he picked up the phone. "Your pops must've been doing about a hundred on the highway."

"He was doing the speed limit." I smiled. It was good hearing Vance's voice and knowing that we were in the same state again.

"I can't wait to see you at school tomorrow," he said. "I miss your pretty face."

"Remember last night…when I said I had something to tell you?"

"Yeah. What's up with that?" he asked.

"It's not good. I hope you're sitting down." I took a long breath, gathered my courage.

"What is it, Tameka? You're scaring me."

"Remember when we did…you know…it."

"How could I forget?" he asked. "It was the best night of my life. Even though I got my butt chewed out when I got home. It was still a special moment."

"Vance, I think I'm pregnant."

There was a long silence. It was as if he'd hung up the phone or something. I knew he was still there, because I could hear him breathing, but there were no words spoken. I needed for him to say something. Anything.

"For real?" he finally asked.

"Yeah, for real," I said reluctantly. I wished it wasn't for real. Wished it was a joke or a hoax, but it was real for now. It was real according to a home pregnancy test. "I took a pregnancy test the other day. The kind you get at Walgreens. It was positive. Also, my menstrual cycle is late. Eleven days to be exact."

"This is pretty heavy for me right now, Tameka. I don't know what to say."

"I know. It's pretty heavy for me, too," I said.

"Is it mine?" He asked those three little words. Words that suddenly ripped my heart apart. Did he have to ask? Didn't he know that I didn't give it up to just anybody?

"Yes, it's yours! Who else's would it be?" I was hurt. Wanted to wrap my fingers around his throat and choke some sense into him.

"I don't know. My dad warned me about girls that try to trap you. Especially when you're trying to do something with your life," he rambled. "I just told you last night that I got a scholarship to Grambling, and now, the next day, you come at me with this pregnancy stuff."

"The only reason I didn't tell you last night was that I didn't want to ruin your night. You were so excited about your acceptance letter, and I didn't want to rain on your parade," I tried to explain.

"I just need to think things through, Tameka," he said. "You got my head all messed up."

"My head is messed up, too. This is not just *my* problem, Vance. This is *our* problem."

"I need to call you back," he said, "I need to think."

There was silence for a moment. This was not how things should be. His response was not what I'd expected. I needed to keep him on the line. Needed to know that he was there for me, that I wasn't in this alone.

"Call me later," I begged.

He never said another word. Just hung up the phone. I'd never felt more alone in my entire life, and I wanted to crawl underneath my bed and never come out. Instead, I cried. Cried harder than I had before, until there were no more tears.

At my locker, I pulled my coat off and hung it on the hook, grabbed my red spiral notebook and my Spanish book. I was tired. I'd stayed up most of the night, wondering if Vance would call back like he'd promised. He hadn't, and I'd finally dozed off at about three o'clock, the Quiet Storm playing in my ear the whole time. Crying wasn't going to change my circum-stances, so I'd stopped that long before 3:00 a.m., but I'd still been wide-awake. My head hurt, and I wasn't feeling Spanish at all. I'd thrown up twice before I'd left the house, and it felt as if I was about to puke again at any moment. Roni had con-vinced me that it was nothing more than morning sickness. Whatever type of sickness it was, I wished it would go away.

Vance approached, wearing a pair of navy-blue jeans and an oversize Sean John shirt. His sneakers looked as if he'd just cleaned them with a toothbrush. He looked just as worn-out as I did, with bloodshot eyes and bags underneath them. He'd graduated from his crutches and was simply wearing a funny-looking shoe on his foot instead.

"Hey, what's up?" he said once he got close.

What did he think was up? Nothing had changed since last night.

"Nothing." I had an attitude. My morning had been just as lousy as his.

"I'm sorry I didn't get a chance to call you back last night," he said.

"Don't worry about it."

"It's just that you caught me off guard and everything...you know, with this whole baby thing," he said. "I needed to think things through a little bit."

"Well, good. I'm glad you had time to think," I said and slammed my locker shut, walked away from Vance. "I don't really have that kind of time. I've got to make some decisions about my life, and I have to do it now."

"If you need money for an abortion, I can probably get it for you this week. I get an allowance, plus I got my dad's credit card."

"I haven't decided if that's what I want to do yet," I explained.

"What do you mean?" he asked. "You're not really considering having it, are you?"

"I don't know yet," I explained. "I don't really believe in abortion."

"You mentioned that you did a home pregnancy test. Have you considered going to a real doctor? Someone who can give you a second opinion?"

"I have an appointment this afternoon at the free clinic," I explained.

"You want me to go with you?" he asked.

"Only if you want to, Vance," I said. "Don't let me twist your arm or anything."

"No...I want to go," Vance stated. "I should be there with you."

Those were just the words that I needed to hear. I needed to know that he had my back.

★ ★ ★

In the waiting room at the free clinic, babies cried and toddlers ran around in soggy Pampers, which needed to be changed. Some woman spoke Spanish to her child and grabbed her by the arm. The woman seated across from us wore a frown on her face. She held an ice pack on her forehead, while the man seated next to her snored loudly, his head bouncing against the wall, as he waited for the nurse to call his name.

"This place is disgusting," Vance whispered. "Why did you come here?"

"It's not like I can go to my regular doctor's office," I explained. "She knows my parents too well. They've been on cruises together. I need to do this privately."

"What if it turns out that you're pregnant? What do we do then?" Vance asked.

"I don't know. I haven't thought that far," I said.

A wrinkle in his forehead, Vance nervously rested his elbows on his knees and intertwined his fingers. I could imagine that his heart was beating at maximum speed.

"Tameka Brown?" the nurse called.

It was finally my turn. I hopped from my seat, and Vance sat still. I gave him a puzzled look, wondered why he just sat there.

"What? You want me to come?" he asked.

"Yeah," I said.

Together, my hand in his, we followed the nurse to a small room, where she handed me a plastic cup with my name on it.

"You can step right in there and urinate in the cup," she said and pointed toward the ladies' restroom. "When you're done, just slip the cup into the little cubbyhole, and the doctor will see you in a moment."

I did as she'd instructed: I urinated into the cup, tightened the lid and slipped the cup into the cubbyhole. I washed my hands and then joined Vance in the examination room, where he had patiently waited for me. We were silent as he flipped through an *American Baby* magazine. I examined the posters on the walls; one of them showed the stages of pregnancy and described what to expect during each stage. After a few minutes, there was a light tap on the door.

"Miss Brown?" said a foreign doctor as he stepped inside.

"Yes, that's me." I gave a fake smile.

He offered his hand. "I'm Dr. Lei."

"Glad to meet you." I shook Dr. Lei's hand. "This is my boyfriend, Vance."

He shook Vance's hand and then took an ink pen out of the pocket of his jacket. Pulled out a notepad and began scribbling something on it.

"I'm writing you a prescription for prenatal vitamins," he began. "You are in your first trimester, of course."

"So I am pregnant?" I asked.

"Yes, you are pregnant," Dr. Lei said. "Seven weeks to be exact. I would like to get you started on the prenatal vitamins right away, and you should make an appointment to come back in about thirty days."

I was in a daze. After hearing the words, "Yes, you are pregnant," I didn't hear much else. As the doctor continued to scribble the prescription for vitamins on the pad, I felt light-headed.

"Are you okay, Tameka?" Vance was asking.

"It's not unusual for her to experience light-headedness, nausea, some vomiting," Dr. Lei explained. "Especially during the first trimester. But it should pass after a while." He ripped the prescription from the pad and handed it to Vance. "Do you have any questions for me?"

"I don't," I heard Vance saying. "Tameka, you got any questions?"

I was somewhere else, in another place…another zone. My head was spinning out of control, and I felt like I needed to throw up. I wanted to lie down, take a nap, and hoped that once I woke up, all of this would be just a bad dream.

Vance held my hand all the way to the automatic doors at the front of the free clinic. We walked across the street to the MARTA station and waited for the train. Once it pulled up to the platform, we hopped on. Vance held on to my hand, our fingers intertwined, as we sat on the orange leather seats. My head on his shoulder, I remained still until the train finally pulled into the College Park station. When the doors opened, we hopped off and walked two blocks to my subdivision.

"Thank you for going with me today." I smiled.

"I'm sorry about what I said last night," he said. "You know…asking you if the baby was mine and all. It was just a surprise for me, and I was scared."

"I'm scared, too," I said. "I don't really know what to do."

"Well, I'll definitely go with you when you have the abortion," he said. "And I'll pay for it, too. Just let me know how much it costs."

There was that conversation again—about abortion, something I wasn't sure I wanted.

"I'm not sure if that's what I want to do."

"What do you mean?" he asked. "You're not thinking about keeping it, are you?"

"I don't know, Vance."

"Tameka, neither one of us is ready to be anybody's parent. You have to know that. And I'm going away to college in the fall." He explained things that I already knew. "And you're still a kid yourself."

"I know all that, Vance. But I don't believe in abortion. It's wrong to take another person's life like that," I said. "There are other alternatives. Like adoption."

"You mean, go all the way through with the pregnancy and then give the baby away to someone else?"

"Yes, to a family that can take care of it," I explained.

"But in the meantime, your whole life will be ruined. You'll have to drop out of school or go to an alternative school. Your reputation will be at stake. Your parents will be pissed off for the next eighteen years," he said. "But if you just have the abortion, you won't have to tell anyone. It'll be a secret between me and you, and no one else will ever have to know."

"I'll know, and it would haunt me for the rest of my life," I said. "My mother had me at sixteen. What if she had just aborted me? I wouldn't be standing here, talking to you, right now."

He sighed. We had reached a crossroads. Neither of us agreed with the other, and we were getting nowhere fast.

"Well, if you decide to have it, I can't promise that I'll be around. I have a bright future ahead of me, Tameka, and I'm not trying to throw it away," he said. "I'm not ready to be a father. I'm not trying to hurt your feelings, but that's the way I feel about it."

As we approached my house, Jaylen pulled up beside us, driving his mother's Toyota Corolla. The bass from the music was so loud, the car vibrated as he pulled next to the curb.

"I told J to meet me here, to pick me up," Vance explained. "I gotta get home."

"Will you call me later?" I smiled. "Not like last night."

"Yeah, I'll call you when I finish my homework," he said. "And you need to decide what you're gonna do by then. You need to let me know tonight."

I sighed. My heart was heavy. Vance had given me something of an ultimatum. If I decided to keep the baby, he wouldn't be around. If I aborted the baby, I couldn't live with my own guilt. But the reality was, I needed to decide one way or another, and quickly. I adjusted my backpack on my shoulder, got a better grip. I pulled my house key out of my Coach purse and unlocked the front door.

Mommy was cooking one of my favorite meals—spaghetti and meatballs. I could smell the garlic, onions and bell peppers throughout the house. For the first time in my life, the aroma made me want to throw up. Things were definitely different. It was like being on a ride at Six Flags, and the ride was just beginning. I decided to secure my seat belt, close my eyes and pray that it would be over quickly.

thirty-one

Vance

AS I lay flat on my back in the middle of my bed, my eyes facing the ceiling, I went over the details of my day. It seemed that I must've had an out-of-body experience, because nothing had seemed real. What had Carver High's point guard been doing at the free clinic with his girlfriend in the middle of the afternoon? I remembered scanning the room the minute Tameka and I had walked in, praying there would not be one familiar face in there and hoping that no one could identify us. All I needed was for someone to see us and spread dirty rumors about why we'd been there—like we had some sort of venereal disease or had just found out that one of us was HIV positive. None of those things were the case, but finding out that Tameka was pregnant had been just as scary. And the thought that she might keep the baby and actually go through the pregnancy— that was downright terrifying.

I was helpless in this situation. We were both in the same boat, but she was the one sailing. She was the one giving orders, making decisions about my future. My suggestion was to end the pregnancy—a clean and swift solution to our problem. That way no one would ever have to know, and both of us could move on with our lives. I could go on to college without any worries, and she could finish high school and remain on the dance team. Our lives didn't have to be interrupted unnecessarily. That would've been my decision, but she had another plan in mind.

I'd dialed her number at least ten times but never hit the send key. I didn't hit it until the eleventh time, when I finally had the nerve to talk. Her phone rang three times before she finally picked up.

"Hey," she said softly.

"What's up?" I asked. "You feel better?"

"Not much," Tameka whispered.

"Why are you whispering?" I asked.

"Because I'm in the laundry room," she explained. "My cousin from North Carolina lives with us now, and she's pretty much taken over my bedroom. My mom's in the family room. My daddy, who's rarely home, is in the kitchen. I had to go somewhere in the house where I could have some privacy."

I sat up in bed, grabbed my basketball from the floor and tossed it in the air. I needed to do something with my hands, needed to get rid of some of my nervous energy.

"Did you decide?" I asked.

There was a long pause, and I wondered what she was thinking, doing. I imagined that she was just as scared as I was, maybe even more. After all, it was her body that was changing—her stomach that was growing. However, my future depended on the answer to that question.

"I'm not killing my baby," she whispered.

The words had me paralyzed. I stopped tossing the ball for a moment and just held on to it, as if holding on to it would change things. As if holding on to it would make the room stop spinning. Didn't she know that she was ruining my future and hers?

"Are you keeping it or putting it up for adoption?" I asked.

"I don't know yet," she said. "I'll decide when the time comes."

When the time comes? What time is she referring to? The time is now!

"I'm going to college in the fall, Tameka," I explained to her. "I have a full scholarship to play ball, and I'm taking my free ride. I can't make any promises that I will be there to help you if you decide to keep it. I don't even have a job. I can't even support myself, let alone a kid."

"Then I'll get a job," she said. "Nobody's asking you to put your future on hold, Vance. You go on to college and do your thing. You don't ever have to even see the baby."

And with that, she hung up. She was gone, and I was left with a million thoughts racing through my head. I had told her where I stood. She had dismissed my plan without any consideration. This could've been so easy, but she had complicated it with her emotions. The baby inside her wasn't even a full person yet. It didn't even have legs and arms—not even a brain. It couldn't think or cry yet.

She was already attached to it, and her decision was made. So was mine. I was standing firm. Tameka was on her own this time. She was being selfish, wasn't thinking of anybody but herself. She would have to find out the hard way that we were way too young to be anybody's parents.

thirty-two

Indigo

saturday mornings came too fast, in my opinion. The smell of bacon hit my nose immediately as I stepped inside the doors of the homeless shelter, the smell of bacon mixed with mildew, that is. It was nauseating, but after a while you got used to it. I took off my jacket and hung it on the coat rack in the day room. Rita and her daughter, Jamina, sat in front of the television, catching an episode of a show on HGTV.

"Good morning, girls." Rita was always bubbly, even in the morning.

I wondered how she could be in such a good mood when she didn't even have a place to live. Not a real place.

"Good morning," I mumbled, barely awake. Saturday mornings were when I usually slept in—until noon sometimes.

"Hi," Jade said and waved.

"You ever watch this show?" Rita asked. "They're redoing this woman's entire house. It's kinda neat how they are doing it, too. She's gonna be so excited when she gets home."

Neither of us responded.

"When I get my house, I'm painting the walls that color right there," Rita continued. "It's gonna be sharp! You hear me? Four bedrooms, two and a half baths, just like I had before."

"Mama, please," Jamina said. Her mother was embarrassing her, and I knew the feeling because my mother was always embarrassing me.

"She doesn't see the vision." Rita continued to describe her make-believe house.

Maria stepped into the day room, carrying two aprons.

"Good morning, girls," she said. "Glad to see you so bright and early this morning. Why don't you head on up to the dining room and get cleaned up for breakfast." She tossed Jade and me an apron. "They're already starting to line up."

Jade and I took the stairs up to the dining room. I washed my hands in the sink in the kitchen and then tied my apron around my waist. Folks were lined up for breakfast like they were at the breakfast buffet at Shoney's. Looking at their hungry faces made me sad. I took my place behind the chafing dish filled with scrambled eggs. Jade stood beside me, a pair of tongs in her hand as she placed bacon onto each plate.

Serving food was exhausting, and the thought of having to clean the bathrooms again made me depressed. It was one thing to clean the bathroom at home; at least there I knew who was using it. Here, there was no telling who was using it. The stench of pee always hit my nose first when I stepped through the doors, and there was always toilet paper everywhere. It was like people just threw toilet paper on the floor just for the heck of it. And the sinks, which had once been white ceramic, were now black and disgusting. Living here would be the worst thing ever.

I filled my bucket with Pine-Sol, some sort of degreaser and scalding-hot water. Even a mixture like that wouldn't take away the pee smell, but I used it anyway. Just as I was reaching for the mop, Maria appeared in the doorway.

"I want you girls to do something different today. Instead of cleaning, I want you to spend some time with the other teenagers in the meeting room. Follow me," she said.

Jade and I followed her to a little meeting room, where at least ten teenage boys and girls sat in a circle in wooden chairs.

"What're they doing?" I asked.

"They're just talking," Maria said. "You don't have to say anything, but I just want you to sit back here and listen. This is a group where the young people can share their thoughts and experiences with each other."

"If we're just sitting down, listening to people talk, how can we earn time for our community service?" Jade asked.

"I will make sure you're credited with time earned," Maria said. "Don't worry about it, okay?"

If she insisted, I didn't have a problem sitting back and doing nothing. Anything was better than cleaning nasty bathrooms. I took a seat in the back of the room, and Jade sat next to me. One of the male Hispanic counselors, Jose, opened the group with prayer, and Jade and I bowed our heads, too, praying silently.

"Okay, let's start with you, Keisha," Jose said. "Let's pick up where you left off yesterday. You were explaining how you felt when you and your mother had to move away from your father."

"It hurt," Keisha said. "A lot. I loved my daddy a lot, but I was tired of him hitting my mother. She didn't deserve to be hit like that."

"How could you say that you love someone who beat your mother like that?" another girl asked. "I hate my mother's husband! He threw us out of the car right there on the side of the road. Burned rubber and never came back for us. We ended up hitchhiking with a total stranger back to our house, and then the punk wouldn't let us into the house. Told us to go find somewhere else to stay." She was angry. "That's how we ended up here."

"She can love her daddy if she wants to," interjected a heavy girl with micro-braids in her hair. "You can still love somebody even when they ain't right. Especially if they strung out on drugs or something, like my mama's boyfriend was. He was cracked out, for real."

Jade and I looked at each other. I wondered if she was thinking what I was thinking. These people had major issues. Nothing like ours. The stories got worse as the meeting continued.

"What about you, Jamina?" Jose glanced at the scared-looking girl, who wore her hair in the shortest ponytail I'd ever seen in my life. She pulled her sweater tighter. "Do you want to talk today?"

I got the feeling that she didn't talk much and didn't have a desire to. She was just fine living in her own little world.

"Come on, Jamina," Keisha said. "You sit up in here every day and never say a word. It's obvious that some stuff is bothering you! Get it off your chest, girl."

"Yeah," said the heavy girl whose mother's boyfriend was cracked out. "We all share our business with this stupid group every single day, and you just sit here like you crazy or something."

I felt sorry for Jamina. Wasn't it enough that she had been through something terrible, whatever it was? Now she was being pressured to relive it, and it wasn't fair. I wanted to go to her defense, but I just listened and kept my mouth shut.

"I'm not crazy," Jamina said softly.

"I heard that you killed your best friend," Keisha said.

"Yep, that's what I heard, too," affirmed a girl with a red bandanna tied around her head. "Pushed her right off the balcony of your apartment."

Tears rolled down Jamina's cheek. Her shoulders were crouched as she wiped them from her face. "It was an accident," she said softly.

My heart started beating fast, and I stopped slouching, sat

straight up in my chair. I wanted to cry, too, when I saw Jamina's tears.

"Y'all were fighting, right?" Red Bandanna asked.

"We were arguing over some stupid boy. She liked him, and he liked me. She thought that I had stolen him away from her, but I wasn't even interested in him. I swear I wasn't," Jamima insisted in between tears. "We were on the balcony, and she pushed me. I pushed her back, and before I knew it, we were rolling around on the floor."

"How did she fall? That's what I been wanting to know ever since I read about it in the *Atlanta Journal-Constitution,*" Keisha said.

"I saw it on the news," said the girl whose mother's boyfriend was cracked out.

"She lost her balance," Jamina continued. "She fell over the balcony. I tried to catch her, but it was too late. I couldn't catch her. She fell ten flights and was dead when the ambulance got there. I loved her like a sister. We had been friends since first grade. We were family. I would've never hurt her intentionally, but we were mad at each other…and…"

The room was silent as Jamina cried.

"Friends get mad at each other every day. They say things that are hurtful, but they don't really mean them. I wish every day that I could have that day back again. I would've told her I was sorry, and that I loved her. And that I was proud of her," Jamima said. "I would give anything to have her back."

Jose wrapped his arm around Jamina's shoulder and handed her a Kleenex. "You okay?" he asked.

Jamima nodded a yes and blew her nose.

"My mom was the only one who believed me, not the detectives who questioned me, not the reporters who had camped outside our house. Not even my father," Jamina said. "He left us. Said it was too much for him to handle. Mom tried to keep our house and worked to make ends meet, but without my father's income, she couldn't do it. The house was foreclosed on, and we had to move out. When they repossessed our car, Mom lost her job, and we had nowhere else to go. So we ended up here, but only until she gets on her feet again."

My eyes were watery, and I wished I had a Kleenex, too. I looked over at Jade, and she wiped tears from her eyes. The entire room was teary-eyed, and I needed some fresh air. I stepped out into the hallway to gather myself. Tried remembering why I was fighting with my best friend, too. It wasn't about a boy, but something sillier—like the dance team. I was mad at my friend because she had succeeded at something. I was jealous of her. Our fight had gotten out of hand, but it hadn't gotten to a point where one of us had died, and I was glad.

Today, when Jade and I stood in the day room, waiting for our fathers to pick us up, we were different. Jamina's story was still stuck in my head, and I was sure that it was still stuck in Jade's, too.

"Sorry about the dance team thing…you know, the way I acted when you made team captain," I said. "I was selfish, and I should've treated you better."

"I'm sorry for snitching on you when you had detention. I could've covered for you if I'd wanted to, but I was just mad," Jade said. "And sorry for saying your butt looked flat."

"Sorry about the fight at Macy's, too," I said. "And sorry for ripping the seam out of your favorite Guess shirt."

"Oh my God, that was the worst part about it, my Guess shirt. You could've ripped anything else!"

"You broke my French-manicured nail." I smiled. "You know a sister can't walk around with bootleg nail. You were wrong for that."

"How can you compare a French manicure to my Guess shirt? You know I can't find another shirt like that, Indi."

"I'm sorry. Dang, you got a red one and a white one, too," I reminded her.

"I think you should give me your Ecko Red shirt to replace it." She laughed.

"That'll never happen, chick." I laughed, too. "But you can wear it with your skinny jeans, the ones you got for your birthday."

"Cool," she said. "I wanna wear them next Friday night to the skating rink. You going?"

"I'm still grounded...until further notice," I said dryly. "Parents are tripping."

Jade's father pulled up outside, and she buttoned her coat up and put her hat on.

"I'll see you tomorrow, Indi," she said and handed me a warm smile.

Just as she walked out the door, I stopped her. "Jade," I called. "I'm proud of you for making team captain. You were the best pick."

"You serious?" she asked.

"Yeah." I smiled and pulled my hat on my head and zipped my coat.

"Later, ugly!" Jade smiled, walked back over to me and pulled my hat down over my face before rushing out the door.

I pulled the hat off my face. "Call me when you get home, heifer!" I yelled and hoped that she heard me.

I had my friend back, and it felt so, so good.

thirty-three

Tameka

It had been almost a week since I'd heard Vance's voice in my ear, since he'd walked me to class or showed up at my locker. I knew he was at school, because I'd seen him in the bleachers after school, checking out the basketball team's practice. Had we unofficially broken up? It was a question that had raced through my mind a million times during those lonely days at school.

As I stood sideways in front of the mirror, trying on a pair of jeans that was much too snug, I checked out my stomach. It was growing, and my hips were spreading.

"Oh my God," Roni said as she reclined on the twin bed in my room. She'd already plastered her Mario poster on my wall, above her head. "You're showing. You know that, right?"

I sighed "Yeah. I can't even fit in my clothes anymore."

"Not to worry," she said, "because anything you can't fit in, I'll be glad to take off your hands."

"Cute." I gave her a fake smile and threw my little Aéropostale shirt at her, aiming for her head. "Can't do anything with that, either. My breasts have gotten so big."

"Thanks. This will look really cute with your black jeans, the ones with the pink stitching." She laughed. "I'll take those off your hands, too."

"This is not funny, Roni," I said. "Maybe I should just take Vance's advice and have an abortion. It's not too late. I heard you can have an abortion up to twenty-four weeks in some places."

"When I was pregnant, I was happy to abort the baby, because of who the father was. I hated him, and in turn, I hated the baby. I couldn't wait to have the procedure and get it over with," Roni said. "But after it was all over, I regretted every minute of it. No matter who the daddy was, it was still my baby, and he or she didn't have a chance at life, and I hated myself for killing it. I still hate myself for having an abortion."

"Did it hurt?" I asked, sitting on my bed across the room from my cousin.

"A little. But I didn't really have any complications. Not like some teenagers. Some girls have major issues, like cervical damage, infection and internal bleeding," she said. "I even read about this seventeen-year-old girl in California who died when she took the abortion pill."

"What's the abortion pill?" I asked. I felt really dumb about this whole pregnancy thing.

"It's this pill called RU-486. When you take it, it stops the baby from growing. It's kinda like having a miscarriage," Roni explained. She seemed so smart when it came to the issue of abortion—like she'd done some research or something. "In this girl's case, she took the pill, and a few days later she started bleeding and had cramps so bad that she couldn't walk. Her boyfriend took her to the hospital, and they gave her some pain medicine and sent her home. A few days later she was dying in the emergency room. Come to find out, there were still pieces of the baby inside of her. She died from an infection."

"For real? That is scary." My heart was pounding from the thought of somebody my age dying.

"You should explore your options before you make a decision, Tameka. This is your life, your body and your choice," she said. "Get on the Internet and read the statistics. Read what other girls have to say about their experiences. Don't let anybody make the decision for you. Not Vance. And not Uncle Paul and Aunt Mel, either."

"I haven't even told them yet," I replied. "I gotta do that soon."

I knew I had to tell Mommy soon, before she started noticing the changes in my body. She knew me too well. She could detect the slightest difference a mile away and was already skeptical about my passing up the spaghetti and meatballs at dinner. I knew it was just a matter of time with her. She would be disappointed, maybe even upset, but it had to be done.

"You want me to do it with you?" Roni asked.

"I might need some moral support," I said and grabbed Roni by the hand. "Come on. Let's get it over with now."

"You serious?" she asked.

"Yeah," I said and headed for the door.

My legs were as heavy as lead as I trotted down the stairs. I found Mommy in the kitchen, loading the dishwasher and wiping down the counters. I stood in the doorway and watched her for a moment as she wrapped the extra garlic bread up in aluminum foil, placed it into the refrigerator. She caught me watching.

"What're you girls up to?" she asked. Her eyes bounced from Roni to me. "You feeling better, Tameka?"

"A little bit," I told her. "We need to talk, Mommy."

I didn't want to waste any time. Wanted to jump right in there and get it over with as soon as possible. Whatever I had coming, I was ready for it.

"I'm listening." Mommy smiled and placed her hand on her hip.

With Roni behind me, I felt a little more confident. At least if Mommy swung, I had a witness.

"Is Daddy here?" I asked. Wanted to kill both birds with one stone. I didn't want to have to repeat this. It was hard enough getting it out the first time.

"No, he just left. Went back to the studio," she explained. "You'll probably be asleep when he gets home. This sounds serious, Tameka. What's going on?"

I wished it wasn't so serious. Wished it was something small, like I'd flunked one of my classes or I'd gotten suspended for fighting. I wished I was in trouble with one of my teachers at school, or I'd wrecked the car, even. Any of those things would be better than this.

"I, uh…" My voice started to crack, and I knew I wouldn't make it through without crying. The tears came so suddenly, I couldn't stop them. They were streaming down my face like a river. I looked over at Roni, and she had tears in her eyes, too. She was no help at all—she was supposed to be strong when I was weak.

"Okay, you're scaring me, Tameka. Tell me what's wrong." Mommy grabbed my head and smashed it into her bosom. "Don't cry, baby. Tell Mommy what's wrong."

"I'm pregnant," I blurted.

There! It was out there in the open. Free and clear. She could do with it whatever she wanted to do. I was already prepared to pack my things. I wasn't quite sure where I would go, but I was ready. Maybe I could hide out at Indigo's house for a few days, and then at Tymia's house for a few days—at least until I found a permanent spot. I was ready for the "I told you so" that was surely coming, too. I was ready for the "I'm so disappointed in you" and the "You know better, Tameka," which she was sure to say.

"I was wondering when you were going to tell me," Mommy whispered as she held on to me.

I leaned back and looked at her like she was crazy.

"What?" I asked.

"Did you think I didn't know?" Mommy smiled. "You've picked up all these extra little pounds, your face is fatter than it was when you were five and you've been throwing up every morning like crazy since we got home from Grandpa Drew's. And you frowned when I told you we were having spaghetti and meatballs for dinner. That's when I knew something wasn't right. You never pass up spaghetti and meatballs."

"Why didn't you say something?" I asked.

"Why didn't *you* say something?" Mommy asked. "I thought we were friends, you and I. Thought we could talk about anything."

"We are friends, Mommy, but you're still my mother. And you trip out about stuff sometimes," I admitted. "So you're not mad?"

"I'm disappointed. Wish you had been more careful," she said. "But we've all made mistakes. I've certainly made my share of them, which includes being in the exact same position that you're in right now."

"I'm sorry for not telling you sooner," I said.

"Who's the father?" Mommy asked. "That little nappy-headed boy that had you all upset that day?"

"Vance," I said.

"What's he prepared to do about it?" she asked. "He does know that this is not just *your* problem, right?"

"He wants me to have an abortion," I said.

Roni took a seat at the kitchen table. Her head bounced back and forth between Mommy and me. She never said a word, just listened.

"What do you want to do?" Mommy asked. "Do you want an abortion?"

"No. I don't. I could never bring myself to kill a baby. I already feel it growing inside me. My body is changing every day," I explained. "But I don't know how I would take care of a baby. I'm still a kid. Maybe adoption would work."

"Whatever you decide, I'm here for you, Tameka. I won't leave you out in the cold," Mommy said.

Those words eased my fears.

"I want to go through with the pregnancy, and then I'll decide if I want to give it away or not," I replied.

"This will change everything in your life. You realize that, right?" Mommy asked. "You'll be off the dance team. You might have to attend an alternative school next fall. And pregnancy is not easy. Pretty soon you won't be able to wear your clothes anymore. You'll be fat, and probably miserable. You'll hate the way you look. You'll probably lose what's his name...Vance. Things will be different."

"I think that once Vance thinks about things, he'll come around." I was still hopeful. "He'll understand why I couldn't get rid of our baby. Once he lays eyes on him or her, he'll see. Just like when Daddy first saw me, he understood why you didn't have an abortion. Right?"

"Your daddy and Vance are two different people," Mommy said. "But I'll tell you this. I don't know what he's thinking or feeling, but we are definitely going to have a talk with him and his parents. You will not do this alone. He will handle his part of it. That's for sure."

The thought of telling Vance's parents had me on edge again. My heart started to pound. "Couldn't we just leave them out of it?" I asked.

"Absolutely not!" Mommy said. "You didn't get yourself pregnant, Tameka. He's fifty percent responsible. We'll invite them over for dinner this weekend. Introduce ourselves and get to the bottom of this. It'll be fine. You'll see."

I hoped she was right. Vance had already stopped speaking to me. He would hate me for sure now, for ruining his life. This plan of action was not going the way it was supposed to. The stuff was definitely about to hit the fan.

thirty-four

Tameka

I couldn't stop my knees from shaking as I sat on the sofa in our living room. The button on my jeans was undone, because I wasn't able to snap it shut. I wore a big sweatshirt and had pulled my hair back in a ponytail. I had changed my hairstyle five times already. Had searched my closet over and over again, looking for something decent to wear, something that wouldn't make me look fat and out of shape.

Mommy had made little hors d'oeuvres and her cranberry punch, which she usually made during the holidays. She'd roasted a chicken and made smothered potatoes for dinner. The house looked nice and smelled like Mommy's juniper breeze candle. She'd taught me how to bake an apple pie from scratch, and I was proud when it came out of the oven golden brown. Roni's task had been to put the rolls in the oven while Mommy took her shower and got dressed. Daddy was working in his office until our guests arrived.

The doorbell rang, and my heart dropped. My knees really started to shake as I sat motionless on the sofa.

"Tameka, get the door," Mommy yelled as she came down the stairs.

My legs were heavy as I made the short walk to the front door, pulled it open. I forced a smile as Vance's parents stood behind him on our stoop. His mother offered a sweet smile, but his father didn't. He just looked serious, probably wondering why I was just standing there looking at them, instead of inviting them inside.

"Hey, Tameka," Vance said.

"Come on in," I told them and then opened the door wider for them to enter.

When they stepped inside, Vance started with the introductions.

"This is my mother, Betty Armstrong, and my father, Dr. Vance Armstrong," he said. "Mom, Dad, this is Tameka."

"Nice to meet you, Tameka." Vance's mother offered her hand for a shake.

"Tameka," Dr. Armstrong said. "Pleased to meet you."

"If you don't mind, can you take your shoes off?" I asked. "My mom is real particular about the carpet."

"I understand." Mrs. Armstrong smiled. "I'm the same way about our carpet, too."

Mommy rushed toward the door, my father not far behind her, as the Armstrongs removed their shoes. My parents introduced themselves to Vance's parents, and everyone retired to the living room. Mommy offered the Armstrongs some hors d'oeuvres and punch. Daddy popped in a jazz CD while they all chitchatted. Dr. Armstrong talked about his dental practice, and Daddy talked about the music business. Mrs. Armstrong told Mommy how beautiful our house was, and Mommy complimented her on her outfit. Vance, Roni and I sat on the love seat and quietly observed our parents. The mood was pleasant.

Mommy went into the kitchen and put the food in serving dishes.

"You want me to help, Mel?" Mrs. Armstrong asked.

"Oh, no, you sit there and relax," Mommy said. "Tameka, can you and Roni help me set the table please?"

Roni and I began placing plates, knives and forks on the dining table. Mommy placed the food in the center of the table. When everything was prepared, she invited the Armstrongs into the dining room. Everyone laughed and talked as we passed the dishes around the table. Jazz continued to play on the stereo in the living room, and the smell of juniper floated through the air.

"Thank you so much for inviting us to dinner," Mrs. Armstrong said, wiping her mouth with her cloth napkin. "This chicken is delicious. You'll have to give me the recipe."

"We're glad to have you, and I will give you the recipe, Betty," Mommy said. "The reason we invited you over is to talk to you about Tameka and Vance, and what we're going to do about their...you know...their little problem."

"Problem?" Mrs. Armstrong had a puzzled look on her face. "What problem?"

"Vance," Mommy said, "you haven't talked to your parents?"

Vance just hung his head. I could tell that he wanted to crawl into his plate and hide underneath his dinner roll. He had had no idea that Mommy was going to bring up the issue of the baby. He'd thought that my parents just wanted to meet his parents, just so that everyone could get to know each other. I could've warned him, but then he might not have shown up.

"What are we talking about here?" Dr. Armstrong asked.

"Well, Dr. Armstrong, my daughter is pregnant by your son, and I thought it was a good idea for the two families to come together, meet and see if we can't figure this thing out together." Mommy smiled.

I suddenly wished I hadn't agreed to this dinner, wished I could change things. It had seemed like a pretty good idea before, but now, as I sat across the table from Vance and watched how his face changed to a different color, I knew it had been a bad idea to invite the Armstrongs for dinner.

"Son, is this true?" Mrs. Armstrong asked.

"Yes, ma'am," Vance mumbled.

"What were the two of you doing having sex, anyway?" his mother asked.

"And without protection?" Dr. Armstrong asked. "We've been over this a million times. You know everything there is to know about safe sex."

"Dad, we did use protection," Vance offered. "It's not a hundred percent effective."

"How do you even know that it's your child?" Dr. Armstrong asked.

Mommy stepped in. "Oh, it's his child. If my daughter says it's his, then it's his. She's not like those little sleazy hoochie mamas out there."

I had to defend myself. "I haven't been with anyone else. I'm not that type of girl."

"I'm sure that you're a very nice girl, Tameka." Mrs. Armstrong forced a smile my way. "But there are a lot of young ladies who literally throw themselves at Vance. He plays basketball—"

"Well, you can rest assured that my daughter is not the type of girl to throw herself at some boy," Daddy said, stepping in. "And frankly, I would like to know what Vance intends to do to handle this situation myself. He needs to step up to the plate and be a man about it."

"Is she going through with the pregnancy?" Dr. Armstrong asked. "There are other alternatives, you know."

"You mean, like murdering the baby before it has a chance at life?" Mommy asked sarcastically.

"My son is in his senior year in high school. He has just received a full scholarship to college," Dr. Armstrong said.

"Prelaw," Mrs. Armstrong bragged. "He's going into Grambling's prelaw program."

"That's very commendable. Congratulations, Vance. You should be very, very proud." Mommy smiled and was as sincere as she could possibly be. "And with all due respect, Dr. and Mrs. Armstrong, you seem like you have done a wonderful job with Vance. I'm sure he's a very nice boy and all that. We're very proud of Tameka, as well. She's been on the honor roll since elementary school, and she had plans of attending college soon, too. But the truth is, they've found themselves in this position…and—"

"We'll be happy to pay for the procedure," Dr. Armstrong said.

"What procedure?" Mommy asked. "She's having this baby."

There was complete silence. I glanced at Roni, and she seemed so uncomfortable and out of place. I felt sorry for her. Wished she didn't have to be in the middle of my drama. She had enough drama of her own. And the way the fireworks were bursting at the dinner table, I wasn't sure how things would end.

"These are children," Dr. Armstrong said. "What do they know about being parents? Absolutely nothing! I know my son is not prepared for fatherhood. I can tell you that right now."

"Neither was I at his age," Daddy said. "But I did what I had to do when my wife was pregnant with Tameka. And we've been a family ever since."

"I can appreciate that, brother." Dr. Armstrong turned toward Daddy, looked him square in the eyes. "But that's not how we do things in the Armstrong family. He's much too young to be a father, and we won't support this."

"You don't have to support it, but your son will take care of his responsibilities. That's not optional," Daddy said.

"I might put it up for adoption after it's born," I said softly, afraid to speak. It was like our parents were the ones having a baby and not us.

Dr. Armstrong stood. "Thank you for dinner, Mel. It was wonderful."

Mrs. Armstrong stood and followed her husband to the living room. Vance gave me a mean mug, rolled his eyes and then joined his parents in our living room, where they all found their shoes and slipped them onto their feet.

"It was nice meeting you, Mel, and Paul." Mrs. Armstrong smiled. "It was nice meeting you, too, Tameka."

"If she decides to keep the baby, we'll arrange for a blood test once it's born." Dr. Armstrong shrugged his shoulders. "We'll go from there. If it's my son's child, he'll step up to the plate. He's still going to college and all that, but he'll do his part. If it's his child."

"Oh, it's his child." Mommy placed her hands on her hips this time as our entire family joined the Armstrongs at the front door. "I believe my daughter."

Dr. Armstrong buttoned his trench coat and wrapped his colorful scarf around his neck. "The offer still stands if she's interested in the procedure. I'll be happy to pay for everything. I understand there's even a pill that the women are taking now. It doesn't even require a surgical procedure or anesthesia—"

"Good night, Dr. Armstrong," Mommy interrupted. "It was a pleasure meeting you."

As Mommy ushered Vance and his family out the door, I wondered if things could get any worse than this.

thirty-five

Vance

DINNER with Tameka and her parents had been a nightmare. This whole pregnancy situation was turning my life upside down. The ride home from their house was the longest ride ever, with my father giving me the third degree from the driver's seat and my mother continuously asking, "How did you let this happen, Vance?" As Ledisi's "Alright" played in my dad's CD player, I focused on the words for the first time. I had never paid much attention to my father's music, which consisted of jazz and old-school, boring music. But as I listened to Ledisi, I knew that she had to be talking about me as she sang the words, "This life can make me so confused, but it's alright...I just wanna run and hide..."

The situation that I had found myself in made me confused, and I wanted to run and hide. I wanted to fall asleep, and I hoped that when I woke up, things would be different. But the nightmare was endless. Tameka's pregnancy was real, and soon the entire world would know. It wasn't enough that her parents and now my parents knew. Soon all our friends would know, all our instructors and possibly my basketball coach—the whole world. I flipped open my phone and decided to send Tameka a text.

Thx a lot, I told her.

I felt as if Tameka and her mother had set a trap for me, and I'd walked right into it. If she'd had my back, she would've warned me. She would've given me the opportunity to tell my parents in my own time and in my own way. But instead, they'd robbed me of that opportunity, and I was angry. Hurt. Here I was, hanging on to life by the skin of my teeth—hanging on to a rope that was close to breaking, while I swung in the balance. The next nine months of my life would be a mystery. And if the DNA test that my parents had insisted on turned out positive, the next eighteen years of my life would be drastically different from the picture I had in mind. I had college and basketball on my mind, not Pampers and formula.

Three weeks before senior prom and my girlfriend was pregnant. And who knew how big she might be by the time the prom actually came around. A lot could happen in a few weeks, and that compounded my problems even more. I wasn't even sure if we would still be a couple by then, wasn't sure if we were a couple at the moment. Situations like this should come with a manual, a step-by-step guide to help a guy like me know exactly what to do. But like my dad always said, "if life was easy, it wouldn't be life."

Sorry, Tameka responded. *Is that all she has to say? Sorry?*

Meanwhile, my life was suddenly in total and complete chaos.

After my father pulled the car into the garage, I was the first one to hop out. I limped upstairs to my room. I needed to get as far away from my parents as I possibly could. I shut my door, locked it. Pulled open my dresser drawer and pulled out a pair of sweats and a hoodie. I changed out of the slacks and dress shirt that I'd worn to Tameka's earlier. Slipped the sweatpants on and pulled the hoodie over my head. Placed a pair of gloves on my hands and headed toward the front door. I hopped down the stairs and into the middle of the street. Crutches underneath my armpits, I moved as quickly as I could. The wind hitting me in the face, I kept moving until I reached the end of the block. I immediately turned around and moved in the opposite direction, back toward the house. Cleared my head.

In my room again, I sat on the edge of the bed, still shivering from the cold. I didn't bother to turn on the television or stereo. Instead, I sat there in complete silence, just trying to find some order in my life again. When I heard the light tap on the door, I knew it was one of my parents.

"Baby, can I come in?" Mom asked.

She didn't wait for an invitation before she pushed the door open and came in. After shutting it behind her, she joined me on the edge of the bed.

"How you feeling?" she asked.

"Confused," I said truthfully.

"I know, baby." She grabbed my hand in hers. "But if it's any consolation, I want you to know that I think Tameka's a sweet young lady, and I believe that the baby is yours."

"So do I," I whispered.

"I understand why she doesn't want to end her pregnancy, too. Abortion is not the cure-all for every pregnancy. She has to do what's best for her," she said.

"What about what's best for me, Mom? She's only thinking of herself," I argued.

"No. She's thinking of her baby, and I have to admit, that's commendable. As hard as it will be for the two of you, she's willing to be a real mother and stand up for her child. She's going to endure the most pain in this, Vance. Soon her stomach will grow, and her body will begin to change. She'll have mood swings and crying spells. She'll go to school, and everyone there will know that she's pregnant. And they'll judge her…"

"They'll judge me, too," I insisted. "Everybody knows that she's my girl."

"They won't judge you as harshly as they will her," Mom said.

"It doesn't have to be this way, Mom. She's making this way too complicated. She wants to carry this baby, and for what?"

"For life, Vance." She looked at me square in the eyes. "She's making the choice for life. Twenty years from now, when your son or daughter looks you in the eye, they'll know that you chose life for them. And they'll thank you."

"I don't understand," I said.

"You will, son. Maybe not today. Maybe not even next month, but you'll understand it one of these days," she said. "But for now, you support that girl. You treat her with respect. She's the mother of your child." Mom kissed my cheek, stood and headed toward the door. "I'm here for you. If you're ever feeling confused again. If you get depressed or just want to talk."

"Thanks, Mom," I said. "I do have a question."

"What's that?" she asked.

"What do I do about senior prom? It's in three weeks," I said. "Do I take somebody else?"

"I can't tell you what to do, Vance," Mom said. "But I'll leave you with this thought. Think of all I just said about what Tameka will be going through over the next several months. Ask yourself how she would feel knowing that you took someone else to the prom, knowing that she didn't get in this situation by herself. Then make your decision. Do what's in your heart, sweetie."

She left me with a lot to think about, but with things in perspective again, I felt better. Life was really about choices, and I had some to make. I just needed to make sure they were the right ones.

thirty-six

Indigo

MY feet on the edge of the bed, I wriggled my toes and then smashed my heels against Jade's leg. She pushed them away.

"Get your feet off me, Indi." Jade frowned. "They smell like corn chips."

"My feet don't smell like no corn chips, girl!" I laughed and wriggled my toes in Jade's face. "They smell like rose petals."

"Whatever, Indi," Jade said. "Guess who invited me to the senior prom?"

"Who?" I asked, my eyes steady on her as she actually blushed. "I know it's not Kendall Keller."

"Yes, Kendall Keller, and I'm going, too."

"That's cool, I guess, as long as you don't take any pictures." I laughed.

"Not funny. Kendall's a sweet guy. Besides, he got a job and a car." Jade relaxed on my bed, her knees pulled to her chest as she painted her toenails. "I don't care what y'all say. I like him."

"I never said anything bad about him. I just can't stand the pop-bottle glasses. Can he get some contacts or something?" I asked. "He's actually kind of cute without the glasses."

"There's more to him than just looks, Indi," Jade insisted.

"Like what?" I asked.

"Like he plays basketball. He's smart. He's nice," Jade said.

"I know. I'm just messing with you. Kendall is nice," I said. "Is he going away to college in the fall?"

"He's staying here. Going to Georgia State. So we might kick it a little bit next year, too," she said. "Marcus will be a senior next year. Which means y'all got one more year left to hang out. And then he's off to college somewhere. What's up with that?"

"Don't remind me," I said sadly. "I'm trying not to think about it right now."

"Well, you better start thinking about it. You don't want something like that to creep up on you. You want to be prepared."

"I'll be so lonely when he leaves," I said.

"No, you won't! You'll still have me to hang out with. I'm not Marcus, but I'm still your best friend."

That was good to know. After all the drama that Jade and I had gone through, I'd felt lonely without a best friend. But upon hearing Jamina's story, my heart had immediately changed. It was a story of best friends fighting over something stupid and one of them ending up dead. That was not the ending I wanted for me and Jade. Jamina wished that she'd had a chance to change things, to go back and switch the events of the story around, to make things different before they came to a tragic end, but in life you didn't always get another chance. But Jade and I—well, we'd had a second chance, and both of us had realized it. And what we'd been fighting over was even more stupid than what Jamina and her friend had fought over.

I'd been jealous. I could admit it now. I'd wanted to be the captain of the team, and when my best friend got the spot instead, I'd hated her for it. I'd been selfish, and it had taken a fight at Macy's and community service to show me just how much. Jade was a good dancer. But besides all that, she was smart, she was a team player and she had character—all the things that Miss Martin was looking for. There was a lot I could learn from her.

"So what you wearing to the prom? Have you and Kendall even talked about colors?" I asked.

"Green." She stood and went to the mirror, walking funny because her toenails were wet, picked up my lip gloss and started rubbing it on her lips.

"Green what?" I asked.

"Green," she said. "That's the color we're wearing."

"Nobody wears green to the prom," I protested.

"Green is cute, Indi. I saw some cute green dresses at Macy's and Parisian. There's a lot I can do with green."

"Green is the color of spinach and sweet peas. Oh, yeah, and baby doo-doo," I said. "Everything disgusting."

"Uh, excuse me! Green is the color of money." Jade smiled as she put eyeliner on her eyes.

"Okay, maybe I can picture that. A sexy green dress with the back out. A little low in the front, showing some cleavage." I laughed. "If you had some."

"If I had some cleavage?" Jade asked, her hands now on her hips. "Oh, I got some cleavage right here." She undid the button on her polo shirt and showed me her chest.

"I'm sorry. I don't see anything," I teased.

The truth was, she had way more cleavage than I had. Mine was still stuck in puberty somewhere, refusing to come out. But Jade, she had just enough. Just enough breasts, just enough hips and just enough booty. She was the right height and the right size. And she liked Kendall Keller, and he liked her. She didn't care who had a problem with it. She didn't care if people liked her clothes or her hair, or if they talked about her behind her back. She was Jade—uncut.

And she was my best friend. Today, tomorrow and always.

thirty-seven

Tameka

A bag of potato chips in between my legs, a bowl of ice cream waiting for me on the coffee table and fresh-baked chocolate chip cookies wrapped inside a paper towel, I gorged. I took a sip of Tahitian punch and stared at the television; tears filled my eyes as the woman on the Lifetime television movie cried for her missing child. Someone had stolen her baby from the hospital, and she was delirious trying to find him. I didn't even know my child yet, but I knew that I would be delirious, too, if my baby was missing.

A Saturday night, and Daddy was at work. Mommy and Roni had decided to catch a movie at the theater. I had passed. Wasn't feeling much like myself, couldn't fit in any of my clothes anymore. My face was fat, and my hair wouldn't go right, and I was depressed. The senior prom was taking place this very night, and I hadn't received so much as a phone call from Vance, let alone an invitation. Hadn't heard from him since our disaster of a dinner with our parents. I saw him at school, but he was always in a hurry—to get somewhere. I was tired of crying, tired of thinking.

He was probably picking up Darla Union at her house at this very moment, placing a corsage on her wrist and posing for pictures in her mama's living room. He and Darla deserved each other. They both cared only about themselves. But I didn't care. Something inside me had changed. I had a baby inside me who needed me, and whether Vance was around or not, I had a responsibility to it.

Speaking of responsibility, our family doctor had warned me about eating too much junk food and not enough healthy foods for the baby. He'd suggested a daily dose of broccoli, carrots and fruits. Feeling guilty, I gathered the potato chips, cookies and ice cream and took them to the kitchen. After washing the ice cream down the garbage disposal, I opened the refrigerator in search of the vegetables and fruits Mommy had stocked the shelves with. She'd gone crazy with fruit juices: there were so many bottles of V8 Splash, she had to store the excess in the pantry. And the fruit basket on the kitchen table was overflowing with oranges, bananas and apples.

Dressed in a pair of sweatpants and an oversize Atlanta Hawks jersey, a silk scarf tied around my head, I poured myself a tall glass of tropical-flavored V8 Splash. I bit into an apple and spit the peel into the trash can. I put a chip clip on the bag of potato chips and placed them back in the pantry. It was time I started thinking about the baby. I needed to make sure he or she had a healthy meal every day. I had even decided that first thing the next morning, I'd start taking those humongous prenatal vitamins that the doctor at the free clinic had prescribed. I wasn't sure how I would get something that size down my throat, but I had to at least give it a try. The baby needed vitamins.

When I first heard the doorbell, I thought I was hearing things and continued to munch on my apple and sip my V8 Splash. But when I heard the doorbell a second time, I knew it was for real. I set the glass of juice on the kitchen table and went to the front window, peeked through the blinds. It was dark and I wasn't able to get a good visual of the car that was parked in front of the house, and I suddenly became nervous. Couldn't think of one single person who would be ringing our doorbell at this hour.

"Tameka," a voice called. "It's me. Vance. Open up."

"Vance Armstrong?" I asked.

"How many Vances do you know?"

It was really him. The sound of his voice caused my heart to flutter. But what was he doing here? Did he have another ultimatum for me? Had his father sent him to tie me up, kidnap me and drag me by my hair to the abortion clinic? I still had a few weeks to spare.

"Oh my God," I whispered to myself. "I look a mess."

I took off running to the guest bathroom, my tube socks making a squishing noise in the carpet. Standing before the mirror, I snatched the scarf from my head and brushed my fingers through my hair. Tried to do something with it, but there was little hope. I was long overdue for a relaxer. There was no time to change clothes, and I wished I had time to put on some eyeliner and maybe a little lip gloss, but there was no chance of that happening. Instead, I rushed back to the front door, gave my hair one last brush with my fingertips, swung the door open. Vance stood on the other side, looking like a dream—which was what I needed since my life had suddenly become somebody's worst nightmare. He was dressed in a black tuxedo with a pink bow tie, a matching cummerbund and pink-and-white Air Force Ones. His hair was perfectly trimmed, and his mustache was lined. He smelled like the bottle of Kenneth Cole cologne that I'd given him for Christmas. What a sight he was.

"Hey." He smiled.

"Hey," I said. "What are you doing here?"

"Can I come in?"

The last time he'd shown up on my doorstep when my parents weren't home, it had changed our lives. That was how we'd ended up in the boat that we were currently in, swimming downstream without a paddle.

"I can't really have company while my parents aren't home," I admitted. I wasn't going to make the same mistake twice in one lifetime.

"I've already talked to your mother, Mel," he said and chuckled. "She told me to call her Mel. Said that Mrs. Brown made her sound like an old lady…"

That sounded like her, all right. She always told my friends to call her Mel. She always told them that Mrs. Brown was my daddy's mama, and she had passed away years ago.

"I asked her for permission to come over here," he continued. "She said it was okay."

I gave him a skeptical look. "My mother gave you permission to come over here?" I asked. "That just sounds like a lie."

"Nah, it's the truth. She's at the movie theater right now. With your cousin, right?" He knew too much information not to have talked to Mommy. "She thought it would be a good idea. Said that you could use the company."

I couldn't help wondering what was going on. I pulled the door open wider, let Vance inside. He pulled a clear plastic carton from behind his back. Inside was a pink-and-white wrist corsage from Publix grocery store. He handed it to me.

"What's this?" I asked.

"It's a corsage." He smiled. "For my prom date."

"I thought you were taking Darla Union to the prom," I replied. "Shouldn't you be picking her up at her house right about now?"

"What made you think I was taking her to the prom?" he asked.

I shrugged. "I just figured that since I'm fat, pregnant and not on your list of favorite people…"

Vance grabbed the carton, took the corsage out. He placed the corsage on my wrist. "Will you be my date for the senior prom, Tameka Brown?" he asked.

"Looking like this?" I stood back so that he could get a good look at my ensemble. "I don't think so."

"You look fine just the way you are," he said.

When Usher's voice rang through the room, it startled me. Someone had turned on the stereo, and the last time I checked, I was the only one at home.

"What is going on?" I asked.

When someone dimmed the lights, I knew that something wasn't right. I was relieved when Mommy popped her head into the room, smiled, gave Vance a wink and then disappeared.

"Can I have this dance?" Vance asked, and before I could respond, he wrapped his arms around my waist and swept me into a slow dance in the middle of my living room.

My eyes staring into his, I hoped he couldn't tell how out of shape I had become. My body was different now. There were bumps and lumps in places where there shouldn't have been bumps and lumps.

"I'm sorry for treating you the way that I did before," Vance said. "I'm really scared about the baby, Tameka. I'm not gonna try and pretend that I'm not. But I know that you're probably more scared than me."

"I am scared," I whispered.

"Um…I'm still planning to go away to college in the fall, but if you let me, I still want to be a part of your life."

I rested my head on his chest, hid my face. I didn't want him to see my tears.

"What about the abortion? What about your parents?" I asked. "Do they still hate me?"

"My parents don't hate you, Tameka. They were just worried about my future. They were shocked finding out about the baby like that. And they were scared, too," he explained. "And as for the abortion thing, I read on the Internet about some of the risks of abortion, and about girls who end up with complications. Some of them have even died. I don't want you to do anything that's going to mess you up like that."

"What about when the baby is born?" I asked.

"We'll decide together," he said. "We have time. If we decide to put the baby up for adoption, that's fine. Or if we decide to keep it, that's fine, too."

"Really?"

"Yes, really. I had a lot of time to think about things. And I know what I have to do. Your father was right. I do need to step up to the plate and be a man. I want to be there for you, if you'll let me."

Vance lifted my chin, wiped the tears from my eyes with his fingertips. His lips found mine, and I pretended that just for a moment I was wearing a soft pink dress to match his bow tie and cummerbund. I pretended that we were in the middle of the dance floor at Atlanta's Marriott Marquis, the place where this year's prom was being held. Usher's voice was bouncing from the walls of the ballroom, and my knight in shining armor was rescuing me from my nightmare.

"So you actually missed your senior prom to come over here and hang out with me?" I asked. "That's sweet."

"I'm not missing anything. I'm right where I want to be," he said. "This is not going to be an easy road, Tameka. In fact, it's going to be hard. I'll be going away to college, and you'll still be here, by yourself. You'll have to face the world alone, your friends, Miss Martin and the dance team. Everyone will know."

"That's all I've been thinking about. I haven't even told Indigo, Jade, Tymia or Asia."

I was still going to dance-team practice every day, as if nothing had changed, but I knew that it wouldn't last long. Miss

Martin spotted weight gain like a cop spotted a criminal. It wouldn't be long before she busted me out in front of everybody. The bright side was, there were only a few weeks left of school, and summer was just around the corner. I already had plans of hibernating through the summer. I knew I would probably gain plenty of extra pounds during the summer, but as long as I stayed in the house, no one would ever know. The fall would be an awkward time. When school started again in August, everything would come to a head.

I still had a few months before I had to face the music. I wasn't looking forward to the next school year.

"Life will get really tricky from here on in," he said. "But I got your back."

"I got yours, too," I told him.

As we danced to an Usher tune, I knew that life as we knew it would never be the same. The road we had chosen was unpaved, uncharted territory, and far from perfect, but I believed that together we could make the journey worthwhile.

Discussion Questions

1. In the novel *Deal With It* Tameka deals with several life-changing events, one event being the death of her grandpa Drew. Have you ever lost someone close to you (a grand-parent, aunt, uncle or parent)? If so, how did you deal with it? What did you do to get past the pain of losing someone close to you?

2. Do you think that Tameka should've revealed her cousin Roni's secret of being raped to her mother, or should she have kept it to herself?

3. The conversation between Tameka's mom and Roni's mom was never revealed. What do you think Tameka's mom said to Roni's mother that made her let Roni go to Atlanta to live?

4. Do you think that Roni's mother was sorry about her husband raping Roni, or do you think she didn't care at all? What do you think she should've done about it?

5. What do you think Tameka should've done about the pregnancy? Do you think she made the right choice in keeping the baby or should she have chosen abortion?

6. Were you happy when Vance showed up in his tuxedo and

told Tameka that everything would be okay? What do you think happened in their lives after that night?

7. Was Indigo being selfish when she didn't congratulate Jade for making team captain?

8. Have you ever been in competition with someone close to you (a friend or cousin) for something that you really wanted? Did you win, or did they win?

9. Should Jade have covered for Indigo when she had a detention, or did she do the right thing by telling Miss Martin the truth? Have you ever been in the position of having to tell on your friend? How did you handle it?

10. Which character in this book would you include in the next Indigo Summer book? Why?